after the kiss

Also by Terra Elan McVoy

Pure
The Summer of Firsts and Lasts

after the kiss

Terra Elan McVoy

Simon Pulse
New York   London   Toronto   Sydney

This book is a work of fiction. Any references to historical events,
real people, or real locales are used fictitiously. Other names, characters, places,
and incidents are the product of the author's imagination, and any
resemblance to actual events or locales or persons,
living or dead, is entirely coincidental.

SIMON PULSE

An imprint of Simon & Schuster Children's Publishing Division
1230 Avenue of the Americas, New York, NY 10020
First Simon Pulse paperback edition January 2011
Copyright © 2010 by Terra Elan McVoy

SIMON PULSE and colophon are registered trademarks of Simon & Schuster, Inc.
Also available in a Simon Pulse hardcover edition.
For information about special discounts for bulk purchases, please contact
Simon & Schuster Special Sales at 1-866-506-1949 or business@simonandschuster.com.
The Simon & Schuster Speakers Bureau can bring authors to your live event. For more information
or to book an event contact the Simon & Schuster Speakers Bureau at
1-866-248-3049 or visit our website at www.simonspeakers.com.
Designed by Paul Weil
The text of this book was set in Adobe Garamond.
Manufactured in the United States of America
2 4 6 8 10 9 7 5 3
The Library of Congress has cataloged the hardcover edition as follows:
McVoy, Terra Elan.
After the kiss / by Terra Elan McVoy.
p. cm.
Summary: In alternating chapters, two high school senior girls in Atlanta reveal their thoughts
and frustrations as they go through their final semester of high school.
ISBN 978-1-4424-0211-9 (hc)
[1. Novels in verse. 2. Interpersonal relations—Fiction. 3. Moving, Household—Fiction.
4. High schools—Fiction. 5. Schools—Fiction. 6. Atlanta (Ga.)—Fiction.] I. Title.
PZ7.5.M48Af 2010 [Fic]—dc22 2009044220
ISBN 978-1-4424-0216-4 (pbk)
ISBN 978-1-4424-0217-1 (eBook)

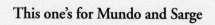
This one's for Mundo and Sarge

Camille

new house #6

pulling in the driveway all you can think is that *this* is the
kind of house they were trying to duplicate back in charlotte:
the real *southern living* deal—a big beautiful old (but newly
renovated) house in an area they are calling the virginia
highlands, with no hills to be seen and two states separated
from virginia. there are brick-based columns across the wide
front porch and a real swing and deep white rockers next
to huge pots—vats really—full of what you are sure will be
hydrangeas come springtime. it's so stereotypical south (and
so very, very far from the noisy cold of chicago) that you want
to laugh, but inside the floors are real, dark, smooth, polished
aged wood—not parquet like in dc or tile like in houston—
and the rugs are just as lush as in the sf penthouse. there are
no long hallways to slide down in your socks like the chicago
apartment, but rooms leading onto rooms opening into other
rooms like a russian treasure box or an alice in wonderland
maze. you cannot believe how much space there is here: wide-
wide everything so wide. how your dad's company finds these
places and what they pay for you to live in them you still can't
get dad to answer, but you are grateful and astonished every
time. this will never be your real home, but it (like the last one,
and the one before that) is certainly beautiful, and you know
your new friends will (like always) be jealous of where you

live, can already hear them (whoever they are) saying *i wish i could be you* in that gushing-awed way that leaves you cold, because no one ever wants the thrown-around rag doll with the threadbare smile. no one wants to be a girl who's picked out her own embroidered heart, string by string, and left it for the birds to tangle in their nests.

new homeroom #5

the eyes have it. seventeen pairs of them already turning as
you come through the door. you could be argus great defender
of juno with all the eyes you have, the eyes you've collected
from all these new homerooms, these new schools, these new
doorways you're always having to step through. you always
wonder what you really look like to them, wonder what it
would be to see out of all those different eyeballs ogling—
green hazel blue brown brown flecked green—to get a three-
hundred-and-sixty-degree view of yourself: forever always
repeating only the surface and never having to look further in.

new french teacher #3

is a man this time which interests you because usually they
are the same type of used-up–looking woman: a woman in a
floral-print skirt with espadrilles or else dansko sandals, with
pale skin that is smooth and soft-looking but also thinning
and with its own share of wrinkles (sometimes about the eyes,
sometimes about the mouth, always the furrow between the
brows), blue eyes usually and long or short hair it doesn't
matter it is always dark and shot with gray. (and if she is blond,
she doesn't have fun.) but no today you walk in (the eyes all
upon you) and you are *bonjour*ed to your seat by a (blue-
eyed, dark-haired, bearded) *monsieur*. tall and smiling (with
wrinkling hands and pink but thinning cheeks) in his floral
tie, he welcomes you with a nod and asks en francaise *how
comfortable are you with the language* and when you answer
back with your prepared little speech about reading camus in
the original french this summer on your own for fun you see
the same little glance of delight you always get with teachers:
like a boy with a marzipan frog that has just leaped to life.

the sunshine girl

new-school day so far pretty smooth. there have been plenty
of curious stares but no one's snickered or snubbed, which
you take as a good sign. two seconds into your third period
though and the bright blonde in front of you whips around,
sticks out her hand like a company CEO and chirps, *hey i'm
ellen. this class is awesome. there's a waiting list so it's amazing
you got in. you're going to love it.* you hear yourself tell her
your name is camille, you just moved from chicago, and then
there's something in the way she's said it—something in her
bright frankness—that just by looking at her yachting good
looks and her hemp-bead bracelets you know that she's right—
that you *will* love this class, and not just because it's about
mid-twentieth-century literature. by the time the teacher starts,
you have programmed each other's numbers. by the time class
is over, she has her arm linked in yours and is showing you
the best shortcut, explaining what to expect from the rest of
your schedule, saying it's weird you're the new girl in their final
semester, but that everyone will love you. that you're going to
have fun. by the time the day is over, you have plans for the
weekend, and—somehow—with nothing like the herculean
efforts required in chicago, the role of atlanta bff is—just like
that—filled.

on being the new girl: atlanta rules

it's not a bad thing that mom aims for smarts, beauty, and popularity in you. be glad for private school and advanced classes and intelligent teachers and the lack of neanderthalism in general. volunteer after school like last time. keep up the appearance, too. as was the case in sf and chicago, being good-looking still makes everyone want to know who you are, which means, at least, you don't have to eat by yourself, and you have something to do on weekends.

interchangeable friends: from chicago to atlanta
bff roxy becomes bff ellen. paula and gregor become jessica
and flip. mrs. haskell is mrs. capriola and mr. fenway is
ms. clary, for sure. betsy is autumn and olive is now connor.
there's a gracen to avoid instead of a stephanie to sidestep,
but also look out for bryce and her flock of straight-hairs.
dorie and willow are eager to include you just like molly
and lucy. sam-paul-jordan-ted in photography class are just
like whatever-their-names-were—football guys, enough said.
and though it's not like you're looking, he-who-shall-not-
be-named is still neither duplicated nor replaced, because
there will never (you are certain you will make sure of it) be
somebody like him again.

New Semester, Same Shit

First period = guitar:
me and
a load of losers longing
to learn Coldplay songs for
the girlfriends they will never get.
Mrs. Fram thinks
we care about her theory
but really we are waiting
until she lets us outside
where we can ignore each other and disappear
in our own strumming.

Period Two = Chemistry II,
and it's unclear how I
learned enough to get here,
here where I keep my head down and my pencil
   moving,
mind fisting with formulas no one else grasps.
Mrs. Baetz and I, we have an understanding—
she concentrates on the other kids skimming
a few dangerous inches below the surface,
helping them get some oxygen,

showing them how to paddle.
Me I am simply stroke, kick, stroke—
gliding through.

Typing = hahahahahaha.
I am in here with sophomores, and that's enough.
Mrs. Ference is
a body filled with fluid,
even the pouches under her eyes.
I am
listening for the squishy noise when she steps.
If she were to be sliced open I know
only wet blistery pus would pour out,
and she would take a long time to drain.

AP History and the walls fall away.
I am
on a magic carpet zooming
along the winds of Mrs. Pasquarelli's stories.
I am lost in the forest of all she says.

AP English next—
my favorite room filled with the smell of dust.
Mr. Burland is tall and strong and ready to lead us
     another semester with his words.
He is the baton for a reluctant marching band,

me the solitary tuba:
important, essential, booming alone.

Math goes in no poem.
Math is a sentence
to be endured.

End the day with econ.
I do not even know what we are supposed to be
    learning here,
but I am gaining
a prisoner's understanding
of the thickness of paint.
Our teacher's ramblings
are an Olympic marathon
and it is a class goal
to distract her daily from her course.
Econ is everything I detest in life
boiled down into four cement walls.
Econ is vapid.
Econ is dense.
Econ is oppressive.
Econ is, purely, dumb.
We do not even
have a book in here.

So there it is—
three hundred and eighty agonizing minutes
all told
until the bell rings and everything becomes
Alec,
lost and counting the minutes too
across town—trapped—
in a different school.

Reunion

Freya flies into the courtyard
gapped-tooth grin wide and high,
overjoyed to be back from holiday break.
How she knows so much
so fast
about so many people
—not just
at our school but over at Seymour and Ivy Glen—
who probably don't know
how to spell her first name
is sheer mystery,
but if there's anyone to know a thing about
Freya will be the one to tell you first.
She's who took me to the Lake House.
And when I met Alec
a month later
I was her fresh gossip
for a week and a half.
But I don't
tell her much.
Her elbows are pointy
and find rib cages easily.

Wednesdays

I like Wednesdays because
usually Mr. Burland is in a good mood and
lets us read parts of our work out loud.
Also we won't have a math test
until Thursday and
there are no chemistry flash cards due.
On Wednesdays I can wear jeans
or a skirt
and neither one means I am being
too done up
or
am just jonesing for the weekend.
Wednesdays are the middle of the balance beam
—they are halfway through the plate of lima beans—
they are you-are-almost-to-Saturday-but
you don't have to have plans yet.
Everyone likes Wednesdays.
(They are betterthanMonday and
notasimpossible as Thursday.)
But Wednesday-oh-Wednesday
you are really my favorite because
there is no such thing as baseball practice and

as soon as the school bell rings I
am in my car and
driving to his arms.

Doing Homework

When I tell Mom I am going to Alec's
to "do homework"
I really am.
But first I will
take my shirt off and he will take off his
and we will lie on his bedroom floor
—the mauve paisley rug, smelling of old fishermen
   and hiking boots—
sharing earbuds, listening
to Kings of Convenience, Iron and Wine, Satie,
letting
our fingers trace each other's rib cages.
Our breaths fall one, then another.
He will roll over then and
lift my giant, over-thumbed Norton—
flip open to a random page of poetry and
just read.
My eyes will roll back in my head, my breath
will swell and slow.
At some point his reading will become kissing me
and the floor will fall away.

Then, after
—and only then—
can we pull our shirts back on,
become mundane.

The Lake House

Saturday night and
you can't see anything the lights are so dim, but
there is a pulse in this party
—shadows shifting off shoulders—
and whenever you catch a stranger's eye it is smiling.
Alec is
with me for what could be all night long
after a week of have-tos,
and clipped-off time.
He is dizzy
and drawling
and I am
not really drinking this beer, just
standing here
talking to Freya
with Patrick somersaulting in the corner of my eye;
   there is
a good song playing
and Eric-Stewart-Tyler
are across the room, conspiring;
a laugh happens in the kitchen right before
—there

Alec's finger in my belt loop,
just—that.
Like the snap of fresh sheets or
the moment your pencil breaks in class it is
so clear and sharp,
I feel it—
his way of saying
Iloveyou
without saying anything
in the middle of the room.

Absence Makes the Heart Grow Fonder

It's not like
I'm ignored.
But at
these weekly parties full of so many people
—some we know and
three-quarters we don't—
sometimes he needs
—*sometimes we need*—
to take a step
and create some distance,
to back off (he says)
and have some space.
There are still
these tendrils between us:
a glowing magical lasso
connecting our eyes and elbows and hips.
When he moves
I feel them pulling me
—even across a room
I'm not in.
Sometimes it's good, allowing a chasm between us,
though I more sense than see him

squinting across the distance.
Still, he knows
I am always here, waving
from the other side.

Secret at the Lakeside

Away from the crowd,
in the marsh and the mud,
he kisses me,
and the egrets
—crouched in dark trees across the water—
are slim white ghosts
in all that black.

Clasped hands,
breathing
we can see the birds
            —dreaming so wildly—
they have to hold perfectly still
just to keep from careening
from the branches.

Hickeys

—are little vampire footprints
telling me
he was here
and
       here.

Camille

the bees

the first few mornings you stand back and watch the dance and buzz of your friends—the bees all flying around and together, looping in wide circles of conversation: flight patterns from flower to flower and face to face, zooming and arcing, together and back, forward and sideways. your eyes swim your head vibrates with the incessant hum of them in all their crazy, complicated backs-and-forths. autumn goes to connor talks to ellen hugs simon with flip moving to dorie then back to ellen who finds simon again, meanwhile willow pecks jessica who flits to parker talking to connor laughing at dorie, while autumn fake-slaps flip then looks at you, with four more bee boys joining in—your teeth tingling with the sound of them. even after a week it is hard to see the center, hard to find the queen—they are all quivering around together and back, this constantly moving-talking-laughing hivemind of smooth clean rich hippie faces, content to weave and walk together, making what you figure must, eventually, amount to honey.

there are no couples

not any that you can determine, anyway: just a lot of buzzing around (and in, and with) one another in pollen-coated, friendswap delight. you know about ellen on and off with simon then sam, and dorie with edgar except when that band guy jack hangs around, and then there's the weird autumn/connor friends-or-more combo, and all the random hookups you've heard about at these famous lake house parties. it's enough to make even you feel like a prude, and then today in enviro science jessica can't shut up about "hanging out" with parker over the weekend, about varsity hot dogs and milkshakes and just driving around awhile, ending up in the hollywood video parking lot unable to disentangle their mouths and hands and parts long enough to go choose a movie, about pining for him since seventh grade, about closure, about feeling complete, about how perfect it is. you cannot believe the grin on her face, the delight in her eyes and the question in yours—*but you and flip?*—because while there will never again be any boy's wrist to tie the balloon of your helium heart to (it has floated high far away from the heavy stone of that unnamable boy in chicago), you would never be with someone and then someone else, and you would definitely never be someone to someone else's else. but here jessica is in all her "empowered" glory, and you are uncomfortable. when

she sees your face she rushes to explain how, yeah, flip is a
little mad at parker but really he has no right because this is
her senior year she should be experiencing everything and if
he really loves her he'll want her to get all her fantasies out of
her system, right? you think yes in some weird way that makes
a little sense—it isn't like the idea is *foreign*—but at the end of
the day you still wish you had put your hands on her shoulders
and simply told her that it's all fine and good if nobody is
really with anybody and that's all okay with everybody, but the
real point should be to be nobody—not to anybody. that's the
whole point.

wandering: atlanta

still not used to a house and not a high-rise, a porch and not
a doorman, but you have to admit the wide-open fresh-air
space is pretty nice sometimes. though that's where you draw
the line. at nice. walking the several long blocks through the
empty (weirdly somewhat green in winter) park along ponce
to school doesn't bug you so much—the time to think or else
not-think is rather welcome, just you and your earbuds and
the one-two of your boots below. it's after school when the
differences between here and there become painfully clear. sure
there are gorgeous, magazine-worthy homes on your street, and
sure it's fun—as always—to look at them and wonder about
the people inside, wonder what kind of lives they're living.
sure too there are shops around—a couple blocks over, then
up from your house—boutiques and gift stores and clever little
restaurants. a homey pizza joint. a dad-worthy beer bar. even
a sweet little gelato place, paolo's—a word you like saying to
yourself: *POW-los*—but after two days of ambling, two days
of gazing into windows and yards, strolling up this street and
that, you realize why you're pacing: there's no coffee place
around here. not one you can get to lickety-quick. there is no
hideout around the corner. no escape. yes, if you make it the
l-o-n-g hike down past ponce, past the "help I'm an AIDS
victim" tranny begging spare dollar bills, and the speeding

traffic and the urban outfitters there's a (okay, pretty cool) joint called the san francisco company, but you can't take yourself too many times to a san francisco that isn't san francisco, and besides you're pretty sure dad wouldn't relish you making that little stroll any time near dark. and anyway you should be able to just walk out your door and practically into a starbucks, or four other indie anti-starbuckses, where maybe they have good danish. this town full of parking lots is no good. though you try to be like mom, try to see each city as a new place full of potential adventure, being unable to walk out your door and be in the midst of all the happenings on the loop, being unable to find good places while staying on your parents' short leash makes it sink in that this is an asphalt prison and you're stuck here for four-ish more months before you can fly free.

the event planner

not even two weeks in this new crazy southern sprawl of a
town and mom has a handful of invitations and tickets and
parks and new things to do and see. it has surprised you
in every city and at this point you'd think it wouldn't, but
once again instead of being unimpressed and exhausted by it
all, she is flinging herself at the experience with wide-open
kindergartner arms. this time no coit tower tours or joffrey
ballet, but a so-so museum called the high. always the major
attractions before she moves on to things with a little more
local color. the aquarium. the coke museum. martinis at imax.
shows at the fox. a thrashers game when she doesn't even really
like hockey. she's a tourist in her own town—these moves we
make are just one big long vacation for her, so why not make
the most of it? she never begs you to go but always *wants* you
to, which somehow makes it harder to refuse. harder to sit at
home. harder to punish her for bringing you here at all.

mystery mail

the magazines, catalogs, and credit card offers have hardly had enough time to catch up with your new georgia address, but even still, today you have some genuine mail, which alone would be enough to give you pause and crook your eyebrow. this however is a real heart-stopper: a regular index postcard covered in duct tape and foil so that the whole thing shines silver in the sun as you stand there in the grass (not ice and snow) by the end of the driveway, stunned to stopping halfway between the house and the curb. five ragged words are scrawled on the back, along with your address. SHINE ON YOU CRAZY DIAMOND, it says. there is no signature, but you know that handwriting. and the postmark's from chicago.

unwanted memory #1

he wasn't supposed to be there. you'd already said good-bye to him—you were leaving the next day for your new house (new school, new life) in atlanta. it was after dinner and you were full of all the things you didn't want to be feeling, all the things that wouldn't let go of you anyway. it was way after his shift at the museum was over, and you'd already pictured him on the el back to wicker park. the morning would be crazy with the movers packing your final few things—the ones that were really yours—so you took yourself for one last coffee, gave yourself an hour of self-pity you didn't really even understand. then it would be time to chuck yourself under the chin, straighten your shoulders, and not look back. there was nothing left but this. it was all already over and gone—so many things you hadn't said and wouldn't now. it burned your throat; it stung your eyes. so when you saw him sitting in the corner there in his scarf you almost turned around, but it was too late—he looked up, smiled at you with a sadness that crushed your heart. it didn't matter—you'd still be leaving the next day, he'd still vanish, you'd still disappear. and yet you sleepwalked over to him, eyes watering. he stood. he held you. you let him. you didn't speak.

care package

walking up the front steps, still staring at your shiny
postcard, you nearly stumble on a package too big for the
mailbox; it is in recycled brown paper bag wrap, drawn with
stars and ponies and girls in tutus, all aglitter with luli's
swirling metallic pens. today wasn't a bad day nor a good
day only yet another day but now it has turned into a hooray
day and a sad day too. luli girl back in sf with her knee-high
socks and her twenty pairs of cowboy boots. her too-short
shorts even in january and the tiny black braids all a-kook
and poking up stiff around her head. luli and her late-night
vespa rides up over twin peaks and out to the crashing coast,
her moleskine notebooks filling up with secret thoughts and
complex codes. there is no girl like luli: not before or since.
you slice open the packing tape and lift out the tinseled
tissue, find a hodgepodge of nothing that is all completely
her: two enameled chopsticks for your hair, one of those
string creatures no one thinks are cool anymore, a mix cd of
"songs for the south," a bag of saltwater taffy and another of
those malted milkballs (*can u git them down theyah?* she tries
to drawl in her scrawl) that she likes but you don't much. a
mad lib she made up for you out of parts of *antigone*, and a
pair of red socks a-moo with purple and green cows. she is
old-fashioned and still likes to write letters, luli, though half

its contents you already know because she e-mailed newer updates before this arrived. still it is like she is there with you, more than a status update or a photo upload, more than an e-mail, more than a call. the couch is strewn with color and sparkle and she is here with you—luli. like always she has followed you to where you need her to be.

Becca

Liberation

every school day is
every unfriendly face is
every long hour is
only a public school tunnel I have to get through
to the light of him
on the other side

In the Volcano's Wake

He places his
fired-iron hands around my rib cage—
Hephaestus' apprentice, moving like lava:
firm and solid—formidable—
and yet flowing graceful rivulets.
Our lips—bodies—meet
as he pours over me—smothering me melting me
so I am liquid and lava too,
flowing with him spreading pushing surging seeing
nothing but orange—
orange orange orange orange orange
and those yellow dots that are
the hot center of a fire flickering.
We are burning everything in front of us.
All is
wavering molten—everything molten—thick with
    heat heavy and searing.
The trees in the forest
burst into flames
as we approach,
dissolving into cinders as we surge surge surge past
burning everything with the power of us,

everything blazing and burning fueled by us
—incinerated in us—surging and flowing and plunging
until finally there is the edge—the ocean—
the abyss.
And we rush to it and drop—   crash
into it then, plunging and swirling down now into
    the darkness,
a geyser of steam and bubbles and the
sssssssssssssssssssssssssssssssssssssssssssssss ascending,
filling the skies—
floating up in billows but simultaneously sinking
    down,
down, down into the cold drifting down,
connecting finally to the ground again,
slowly letting ourselves be cooled,
becoming smoothed
and re-formed.
The edges of me disappear—
the edges between us disappear and I
can't feel anything except where his hand
is in my hand
or where our stomachs are together ribs matching,
mouths one mouth.
In the steam wash I really am breathing his breath;
my heart really is his heart, beating.

First Game

The trees are still sticks of winter,
my breath a white bird
flying from the cage of my ribs.
January isn't done with this field
but here I am, watching
the first stretches of spring.

Cold metal seeps
from my jeans to my bones—
not even the grass will show its green face.

The dry air steals sound
before it is heard;
only the shapes of noise happen
—and one long whistleshriek.

Out here
it isn't hard to remember
teacup cocoons,
sleeping bag saunas,
and the coze of lake fires over break.

White on gray, the figures
bend and snap with action.
The sharp crack of a bat
is like slabs of ice, unhinging.

Baseball season
has begun again.

The Catcher

The only one
looking out
instead of in—he is
hunched over the plate: handsonknees,
eyes shaded but squinting,
watching—a panther—
the moments beneath the movement.

Only I know
inside him—haiku swimming.
Those old-soul eyes
see in sevens and fives
—counting syllables on top of strikes—
looking to the day when he is free
to follow
his true heart in classrooms
which this athlete's body will pay for—
invisible poet,
deep watchful creature of sinew and silence.

Goodnight, Sweetheart

Homework/tomorrow's prep/bedtime routine complete
and I am
sliding into quilt-blanket-pillow-land
when the bedside phone beeps: *You awake?*
His own phone doesn't even ring when I call back,
 it's just
his voice there, quiet,
cozed down in pillows too:
Sorry I had to leave so fast
after the game. The guys were hungry, so—
And I'm so quick to answer with understanding,
that I'm not sure
I sound as sure
as I wanted to try to sound.
Team camaraderie is as vital
as team competition.
I know he has a role to fill,
someone else he has to be.
And I get it, I do.
I get it every time
he thumps them all on their backs
instead of reaching a dirty hand

out to me.

We'll make it up this weekend, he growlish-purrs,
and—like that—his voice is a wildfire
burning away everything,
scorching and searing only one thought
down to my bones.

Time to Get Started

First writers' forum meeting of the new semester,
and now there is no more
get-to-know-you sniff-out;
now we are seniors
and we are in charge:
a literary band
—a flock of formidables.
Now is our time
to make decisions.
To make flyers.
To take submissions
to prove ourselves.
There is no room for
Sara's kohl-rimmed eyerolling,
Rama's heavy-bored sighs,
the freshmen's giggling insecurity
or Charlie in his too-big jeans playing
existential devil's advocate.
It is time for us to really get going somewhere.
It is time for us to do our thing.
It is time to make a magazine.
It is time to unleash the secret weapon.

It is time to press go.
It is time for us
to show this sorry school
what it means to be poetic
what it means
to feel with meaning.

Seventeen Reasons Why

Out of school once again and I can
finally turn on my phone
wait
the agonizing seconds
to see what beeps in.
I am
already on my way to the parking lot
—Freya in tow—
turning the ignition and
revving my way out of here:
off to errands
instead of another baseball practice,
keeping my points in mom's favor
on the high side—keeping my curfew
as late as I want.
Still I thrill
at that little digital envelope: its beep and its blink.
Still my breath
catches,
and I flush
reading his lunchtime composition,
his illicit thoughts

meant just for me:
tired and sore from
six AM practice—the ache
for you is greater.

The Empress of Gossip Magazines: To Freya (with apologies to Wallace Stevens)

Call the pourer of cheap buzzes,
The tipsy one, and bid her whip
In the bedroom scraps of scintillating secrets.
Let the bitches dawdle in designer dress
As they are used to wear, and let the boys
Bring Blow-Pops wrapped in last month's *Us Weekly*.
Let pure escape be the answer to "or not to be."
The only empress is the empress of gossip magazines.

Take from the shopping cart of distraction,
Lacking the three un-wonkie wheels, that glossy stack
—from which she embellished fantasies once—
and spread it so as to cover her freckled face.
If her poorly pedicured feet protrude, they come
To show how silly she is, and dumb.
Let her lip gloss be her only gleam.
The only empress is the empress of gossip magazines.

The Accident

Ten minutes in Target with Freya turned into
an hour, so already we are late,
but this songissogood; turn it up; Christ could the
   light be any shorter?
Don't forget unsalted butter on the way home
Mom said, but
I should text her to see if there is anything else.
Ohmygod go go GO oh god now I have to get in
   that other lane—shit

—Wait—
Where did that—
Why is everything too slow how did
my car my car
[What was that noise did I really *hit* her?]
My god my foot won't stop shaking
and Freya is screaming for no reason.
Wait.
What?
What just   —ohmygod.

Here is the lady at my window.
Do I get out now she—looks so angry.
Next to me Freya says *holy shit* and I say
shut up.

It wasn't my fault.

I should get out now she
—*No I'm not hurt*—
Butmyfootwon'tstopshaking

How did
my car
end up smacked into hers.
What happened who was driving where is mom
my foot won't—

—The lady's cell phone is pressed against her skull
these cars full of staring, angry eyes—

Your fault this is YOUR FAULT!

Don't say anything; don't cry it is
not that bad.

Her brake light is—
and my headlight will never—
I wasn't even going that fast [did my foot slip
off the pedal? it won't stop shaking] she
wants my mom's name here now are
the police.

—The police!—

And Freya is crying—but she isn't the one in trouble.
   Where is that
insurance card my
driver's license is here—

All those staring eyes,
what happened it was only one second I don't know
oh god look at my *car*—!

I'm not dead but my mom will kill me
I'm not dead but my mom will kill me
I'm not dead but my mom will kill me
I'm not dead but

Camille

the puppy palace

immediately there's the smell of animals in closed spaces,
and urine, and desperation—even though this shelter is
small and so friendly—and you take your initial big sniff to
get yourself used to it even out there in the reception lobby,
while your ears ring with the bouncing echo barks of play and
need coming from down the tile hall. the coordinator who
greets you is a once-thin woman turned soft: one of those
short-haired, not-lesbian-but-not-with-a-man-either women
who has reached the point in life where she understands she
likes animals better than people. her name tag says lily. she
reminds you of your elementary school librarian, the one in
phoenix who gave you *love that dog* and changed your life
forever, even though you can't remember her name. you shake
her hand. you hope she finds you satisfactory. there are forms
for you to fill out, copied badly on blue paper. you wonder if
she thought you might be older on the phone, since she asks
if you're from emory. she seems eager enough to have you
though, despite the permanent frown between her eyebrows.
she takes you back, shows you the open play yard and the
big-as-they-can-manage kennel cages. the dogs are all a-bark at
the sight of you: some of them eager, others questioning. you
coo and shush them as you walk. you assure them that even if

you don't stay, even if you don't take them home, while you're with them you will be sweet. you will make them (you will make yourself) forget—for two hours every thursday—just exactly where they are.

thrift shopping with ellen

you think she is joking at first when, after asking you to go
shopping after school with her, she drives you to the biggest
thrift warehouse you have ever seen. sure she's all bohemie chic,
but you didn't think she truly slummed. after all this girl is so
smooth and soft and clean she looks like she was carved from
taffy. her house is a four-story antebellum southern sprawl
and she drives a brand-new mini cooper. she will go to yale
on legacy. consequently you'd been looking forward to getting
up to phipps in order to further costume up and fit in around
here. pre-worn, over-washed, manhandled garments from a wet
newspaper–smelling, fluorescent-lit bargain barn? that's luli's
scene, not yours. still ellen is like a piranha at a cow's carcass,
piling your cart with old secretary blouses and men's seersucker
pants. four trips to the dressing room (at least there is one)
later and she has dropped $167 on three garbage bags full. you
are holding one sad, lone purple nylon cami and insist, next
time, *you* drive.

things to miss about san francisco #12

the pain and stretch in your calves, going uphill. chinatown on a saturday morning, early. zooming across town in luli's mom's gold convertible. marketing with dad—bundles of fresh produce and a whole fish. big bowls of coffee. golden gate park (still). coit tower late at night—supposed to be home soon for curfew. popcorn tossing with sonali. being happy as a family and thinking we might actually stay this time and that dad would just go back to teaching instead of this corporate pop-up tent movearound work-hard-then-go-work-hard-somewhere-else life. ghirardelli mermaid fountain that time with fritz. luli's pigtails so straight and soft and black. science lab with mr. porter. slumber party at sonali's with luli and feeling something like belonging.

things to miss about san francisco (revisited)

funny to look back just now and see how much of "things to miss about san francisco" #1 is so all about people and teachers and rooms full of bubbling faces and projects, everyone laughing and laughing and doing their creative things, when what you really miss now—in this new space with so much space—is the *space* you had there: the free-roam of the park, the wide sidewalks of downtown, the high-ceilinged storefronts and open-happy faces on the street—even the crazy homeless with their piled-up carts. that's what you remember now, anyway, in contrast to what you are also missing about the city that came after it: the closed-in concrete and cold-weather hunching of chicago; the anonymity of a busy street corner; the isolation of a thronged museum. there (in sf) you were open and free and wild and then there (in chicago) you were closed-in and quiet and held close, but quiet in a way that meant thoughtful, that meant growth. now here you are both quiet and closed-in, but the walls have expanded and there is so much room. too much room. room for only you and your thoughts and the paths they trace, leading—always leading— back to the one room (his room) where you felt more free and more intimately closed in than you have ever, ever been.

virtual sleepover

say good night to mom and dad—curled up together watching tivo'd episodes of some dancing show. you will leave them to their being-restored romance; you've got your own date to catch. plunge on the bed and there is luli on the phone—right on time. her actual voice takes a moment to get used to: replacing gchats, status updates, and scattery e-mails—those loose connections you've been able to keep as you've transplanted yourself even farther away from her. luli the exception who proves the rule, luli who wants to know everything—just like when you got to chicago: *describe the wallpaper—who are your new friends—how many blocks this time to school.* she's seen the 360-degree photos you uploaded of the house (*it's so martha!*); and it pleases you she can kind of feel at home. three hours behind your own time zone, she could still go out tonight. it's friday. she has other friends. instead here she is curled up on the phone with you, her questions so constant you can hardly keep up. on opposite ends of the country, you both paint your toenails while you try your hardest to mimic autumn's drawl, and she grills you about teachers and the closest grocery store. when she asks about the nameless boy in chicago, before you know it you have lied: *i don't know.* it is hard though to hide from luli who laughs. luli who lifts, shining her light on your life so you see it in new ways: not a town to dread but one to discover. it is three hours before you hang up with her. three hours before you really notice she's not here.

countinghouse

you are so nervous and excited that your hands and upper
lip start to sweat. hidden in plain sight on the bottom of
your bookshelves, it's always so sweet to lift out. puff-painted
photobox friend—some rhinestones have chipped off but
all those cheery 5th-grade farewell signatures are still intact:
michelle or *daniel* or *nice knowing ya!* on the outside it is your
mostly forgotten past but inside is your own real future, the
one you will make for yourself in europe, the one no one will
tell you how to live, where you will go absolutely only where
you want to for a year, and not where everyone expects you to.
your hands sweating more just thinking about it—those stacks
of twenties, the crisp fifties that have barely seen the light of
day. so hard to make yourself wait a month sometimes—how
often, exactly, since leaving chicago, have you been plied with
more forgive-us allowance? three? five? it could be a really
big haul today. what did you do the obligatory spending on?
new school clothes and treating new friends to treats so they
stay new friends . . . that cool embossed collage with mom at
youngblood . . . *ohmygod just count it already!* so you lift the lid
and it's like you can already see it: your private jet plane. your
magic carpet. your independence and your prison break. only
seventy-something-odd days until you can move around—fly
around—jet-boat-train around—leave. leave on *your* terms,

your own way, not even with a map, or a post-grad college routine, and carrying only what your backpack will fit. it is almost here and your hands won't stop trembling. you sing to them, your squirreled savings, stroking them with a pleasure that tingles up your fingers. you should be cloaked in purple velvet and ermine, a heavy crown on your head. yes, the king was in his countinghouse counting all his money. but no blackbirds will come and pluck anything from you. you will make sure of that.

Becca

Sweet Relief

The chaos of the accident still
shakes my bones,
and blurs my vision.
My pulse
is a small child
running
from a too-dark room.
My mouth says
I am okay to everyone
around the frayed iron bands of fear
still constricting my throat.

A haven of
shower,
pajamas,
macaroni and cheese.

I can forget, almost
—if I don't look out the window
at the carport—
if I walk quiet circles
around my disappointed mother.

My phone blinks—civilization
finds me again.
(Likely my brother,
telling me *nice work*.)
But instead of wincing, I get to smile, am reminded
there is more in my heart
than guilt
and fear.
The envelope blinks:
the saints were watching,
keeping you safe. I light them
one thousand candles.
I kiss my phone, hope
somehow it reaches his lips.

Mom Hands Down Her Verdict

The punishment
for my car-wreck-crime
is an iron door sliding down.
I offer up my neck.
It could be chains
or drowning
or starvation—
the worst being
solitary confinement.

The judge speaks.
I let out my breath,
trapped between
a Scylla and Charybdis of disappointment.
No head on a pike,
no burning at the stake,
but instead—
Debtor's prison.
Forced labor.
For every inch to be repaired
somehow a mile of minimum wage
must be paid.

Sympathy From the Devil

A whine still hangs
from the tip of my voice.
Brother on the phone, dispassionate—
his unfair judgment is
a recent stranger in the room.

A grunt of dismissal—six small words:
Ask dad for the money, then.
And the memories swim up—the shirts left hanging
   in the closet,
the charcoal grill abandoned in the yard,
two boxes
of books
no used bookstore would take,
and a guitar case full of promises
not even a saint could keep.

I can't sigh loud enough
to blow away what he has said.
The pause I take I hope is enough distance.
Bootstrap time, I feel myself saying eventually—

wishing I had
even enough money of my own right now
for some actual boots.

Bitter

When I say
I have to get a job, Alec says
That could be cool, and though
I agree in ways I have to point out
But how will I see you—
and it is hard to swallow
—it is hard to smile—
around the unexpected bitter taste in my mouth
when he sighs sweetly back,
Why do you have to freak out so much?

Carpool with Freya

Four-hundred and eighty-two
Diet Coke cans
crushed around my feet.
Ninety-six
crumpled bags
of Chic-Fil-A
in the back.
The speedometer racing
twelve mph
above where it should be.
Eighty-seven megawatts
of Kelly Clarkson
at seven AM.
Thank God
this is only
until my car's out of the shop.

The Interview

Usually my neighbor Emmett is in
football-watching-with-the-guys or
supper clubbing date-with-wife wear while
I am bouncing Baby Hendrix on my hip and
listening to his wife remind me where
the flashlight is, what the
emergency numbers are.

Today though he is all coffeehouse-owner business:
khaki pants
white shirt
olive green fleece, brown rubber clogs.
His face tries to pretend
I don't know
where the good snacks are in his pantry or
what magazines are in the rack
by his toilet.
He even shakes my hand.

First a tour:
Counter #1 (coffee, espresso, and pastries)
Counter #2 (wine and beer)

Coffee bean wall (grinding and dispensing)
Patio #1 (glassed in, with a real fireplace)
Patio #2 (open air, for the smokers)
Bathrooms
Storage
Office
Kitchen
Outside trash
Back inside to sit together on the couch
by the window.

It is
too much like Dorothy and the Scarecrow
    in their movie:
I've seen you before but somehow never seen you.
Am I to pretend
I haven't been here,
haven't
hung out at that table right there with Freya,
that I don't know
the vegan pumpkin muffin is the best?
Do I call him
—today—
Mr. Siegel?

The questions rush out of his mouth:

Can I handle cash?
Can I multitask?
Have I ever stolen from an employer?
Do I have an interest in coffee?

I am honest: yes, yes, no.
And does it count if I have an interest
in learning whether or not
I am interested in coffee?
I have cleaned his child's vomit
out of my hair!

His handshake is a meat sandwich.
He shows me Paige and Stan,
whose coffeecool eyes think
I am in kindergarten,
and whose wan smiles suck out
all my excitement
hearing my new boss explain to them
I will start tomorrow.

First Day at Work

Even though I am
taller than the two college girls I meet, their slim
   pixie faces believe
I am eight kinds of small.
Driad nymphs, their deft white hands
fly with money and espresso moving through them
like silk.
They are
tattoo-waisted and ankled
with thrift store sweaters and beaten-in shoes.
I am
in their way most of the time
in my blistery loafers and my
J Crew trying-too-hard turtleneck.
For two hours I watch
and listen,
am shown things I beg myself not to forget,
watch people and take mental notes
I can't wait to share with Alec.
My head hurts;
my ankles hurt;

my eyebrows hurt.
Is it mercy or a bad omen—
eventually me, on a stool, rolling silverware until
    shift's end.

Comedown Letdown

The cold air is making
the stars twist in a velvet sky, dancing
themselves to sleep.
It is the loveliest thing
—the first of fresh air—
I've seen all day.
Home, almost midnight,
my call goes to him—wanting
to say everything,
to hear one last good night.
Nothing seems real
unless I share it with him, but
three rings and his bleary, baseball-worn voice
is not sure who I am.
When I say *I did it*—
my first day of work.
He only asks
did I get him
any free
croissants?

Camille

so many puppies

you haven't even been in the shelter for two minutes on your first real day and already the puppies are all dying to go home with you. they wriggle and jump and squeal and beg—their thin little legs stretching up, noses sniffling, wide eyes roving all over your face, sending out their messages of longing *lovemeloveme!* while the other older dogs only look to see what the puppies are looking at. it's the semi-new ones—the ones who still remember what it's like to have a home—who give you the saddest deepest most knowing looks, the ones you truly ache for. these tenants are only curious about your new smell and what you might give them but largely they are not impressed. they have seen the likes of you before. they may be intrigued by the looks of you, but they know that you—like everyone else—will leave them in the end.

spaz attack

you'd think the president was coming to campus this morning,
the way everyone's sweating. even ten yards from the building
you can feel the nervous energy pulsing—some kind of frenetic
force field that it takes sheer vulcan mind power to punch
through. *they're hardly interviewing anyone—did you hear*
chelsea got called?—they've got a multiple-choice exam with them
harder than the GRE—the one with the tie speaks six languages
at least: all snippets and half-thoughts you catch on your way
to meet ellen, who herself seems to have turned an even whiter
shade of pale. recruiters, apparently. from harvard, princeton,
and brown. here interviewing "top candidates" who applied
last semester. dorie's getting out of her music theory and
interpretation class for them in two hours, and she's going to
need to take something if she doesn't calm down. ellen fans her
with a folder and helps her run through her prepared answers,
but it's hard to stand there and not want to knock dorie over.
when you say so to ellen under your breath, she looks at you
like she just sniffed sour milk, and then at lunch when even
flip is flipped out about essays, because early-decision folks
are all chosen by now—*she's going to get a scholarship*—they
think he could test out of lang—suddenly your cavalier attitude
feels a little dragged behind a horse. your freedom feels
fabricated. your detachment *déclassé.* though the hysteria's a bit

annoying—though the drama's half *crucible* in its crescendo—if you cared about college yourself then at least you'd be in their conversation, you'd have more than two acceptances for show, an unanswered "safety" application to berkeley, and a shoe box full of dollar bills.

mystery mail #2

this one's a watercolor. perhaps it's a gargoyle, maybe it's a mound of stones on the front—it's really too blurry to tell. lots of varying shades of gray and a streak or swirl or two of blue. on the back, scrawled in pen, near the bottom left corner: *you are a stone fox*. this is from one of your favorite scenes in *the virgin suicides*. there is no signature. the postmark's from chicago.

unwanted memory #2: first sight

he caught your eye right as you first walked in, and you couldn't keep your eyes from sneaking back to try to catch him again: tall-tall-tall and cheetah lean, with skin the color of egypt, heavy black eyebrows and curls (moppy on top, short around the sides and back), and a white white smile that he pulled out like a bouquet from a magician's sleeve as he greeted each new person in the coat-check line. you had never seen such a boy and your eyes could not stay away from him as you stood behind mom, pretending to admire the— um—ceiling while you waited for tickets, looking behind you where sightseers and art students moved in through the main doors. every time you snuck your glance at him though—every time—his own eyes were just darting away. so you weren't sly and suggested that mom check her jacket—just a light little tweed thing; it was still summer then—trying to count the number of people ahead of you, to see if he'd call you next. you don't remember what he was wearing that day but you are picturing him now in the striped gray slim pants and the nubby wool sweater, the art institute badge around his neck, along with his collar and tie done in that way that made him look british instead of preppy. above that the firm hard knob of his adam's apple (oh that adam's apple, the sinewed hollows of his neck) worked up and down over what he would say to you the *fourth* time you came in, after it was clear you were going to have something to check each visit. when it was clear this had become a habit.

these parties

have ever only served one purpose: drink to mouth and then
mouth to mouth, from the beginning of time. it doesn't matter
who you are or where you are: what city, town, or country.
when you are beautiful and young and bored you will flock
together like beads of mercury. here conditions are particularly
ideal since this town's host is—at least you've heard—no one's
best friend, only a rich kid college dropout party boy who's
still trendy with the teens but too odd for his own kind. so as
the weekend turns its lazy corner toward you, the messages
get sent and the radar is detected and everyone spends all of
friday going *who-will-drive-us-what-will-you-wear-is-she-going-
what-time-will-you-get-there*, and just like in charlotte where
everyone was everyone else's business and there wasn't anything
else for anyone, you are swept up and dressed up and carried
away. these-jeans-not-those and definitely not a skirt. that-
top-no-this-one because it's warmer than it looks. ten minutes
until willow arrives to pick you up and you almost chicken
out—mom's not asking but you can feel her excitement for you
buzzing up the stairs; she'd curl up with you and a movie in a
minute though—maybe it's safer to just stay in. but then even
just that idea in your head makes you suddenly a desperate bird
in a cage, beating wings to be let out. the doorbell rings and it

is time to go. you smile as mom smiles at willow-edgar-dorie just inside the doorway. you are not sure you are (will ever be) one of them but just like always your coward heart wants to make sure she is the only one who doubts.

ellen explains it all

leaning against the cool smooth stainless steel of this stranger's refrigerator—you have not met the infamous host (are unsure even how many people live here, besides the two bong-eyed college kids collecting fives at the front door)—you are sipping only tonic, and are here only because it's where all your friends are, where everyone seems to be really: even everybody from everywhere else. although you are tired of noting faces, keeping track, paying attention, pretending to listen to these anybodies who will turn into nobodies in a few short months, you are still standing here and you are still watching everyone who comes in. it's like ellen's reading your mind then, because she rolls her already-bleary-blond head over to look at you, waving her cup in the general direction of all these nobody/everybodies both here and beyond, explaining, *this is what it's all about, man. we won't be here much longer. so crush as many people against you as you can. soon they'll be gone. and we'll be gone too. but if we experience everybody, maybe somebody will remember.* she clinks her cup with yours and gives you a lopsided half-sad grin, and though you feel yourself already becoming a nobody—though she'll never know (oh how well you know) the people you've crushed—this minute she just made you her somebody and you are both glad.

the surprise

he comes into the kitchen, and before you've even thought
twice you're asking ellen who he is. when she tells you he's the
catcher for seymour high's nationally ranked baseball team
you aren't the least surprised: he is a pyramid boy with atlas
shoulders and merman hips—a boy with muscle to spare. he
is a quick boy—moving to one of the coolers under the table,
fisting a mouthful of chips—but not a fast one: the ease of him
almost too easy, everything about him actually *too* and *easy* as
you're looking-not-looking at those glossy curls thick enough
to balance grapes, the toothsome smile, the heavy hands that
stay shoved in pockets while he talks. only thirty seconds in
the room and everyone is moving around him like it is their
birthday and he is the cake, even the other guys, the shorter
soccer guys, the baseball-capped groupie guys and even those
from tennis and track. he is stay-away-from-me handsome,
likely all gimme hands and grabby mouth—one of the ones
who knows so much and about whom you know lots better.
you can spot them coming a mile away like a slowball high and
to the right: this one no different with his chisel-chin-chin,
except when he turns his eyes toward you its not a slowball
but a curve—his soulful eyes a mirror that shows your own
solitary reflection.

hooking up

not sure what time it is anymore—the room is full of smoke
and mirrors but you could navigate it blindfolded, not a
flitty bee but a smooth shark who needs no eyes, constantly
moving and seeing with the edges of your fingertips, elbows—
sensing with your earlobes. you are restless and it is time for
something to happen. this one will not do and not this one
either, too-tall/too-short/too-loud/too-just-too much leering
there in the door frame. there is music you don't like but
don't pay attention to—it's all part of the vibration of the
current by now, what keeps the kelp swaying and what keeps
you camouflaged. twice around the room, one time more (so
many rooms, so many rounds, you cannot keep them straight
anymore only a curved glass barrier against which you pace).
your glass was half-empty and now it's half-full of something
that vaguely tastes like rum. a friendly face you know swims
before you, pale pulsing jellyfish aglow against the dark. the
pyramid boy with the mirror eyes has disappeared but you are
glad—there are simpler fish to shoot in this barrel. his name
is josh his name is matt his name is kristopher his name is
astrophel—it doesn't matter you only have to say it once. the
smiling is the rest: that tender hooked worm that he will soon
snap and swallow whole. there is a cove there is a room there
is a corner there is a hallway there is a place you go where it

is dark and for a moment—when he doesn't speak—where it is quiet. it's there everything will be silenced and stilled and forgotten, only one mouth on the other, one hand in another fist, one body against another body and all the nattering talking remembering thinking parts of your brain dissolved and dismembered in a swirl of salt. there is only the fish brain working now, only the part of you that is octopus. the part that is disappearing now in a cloud of ink.

Sunday Morning Shift

Bacon-egg-cheese biscuit
two coffees here is
your change (seventythreecents). Nadia brings
Good morning what can I get you?
another basket of croissants from the back;
—Yes ma'am here is your bagel the toaster is over
    there, here
More coffee? Refills are—how much?—
ninety-eight cents
plus two muffins equals three
ninety-one—no four—my feet
are killing me already
Good morning what can I get you?
even in these new shoes. There's the phone ringing I
    hope someone else can get it
—slice the bagel—what are the herbal teas again?—
    Here you are, sir.
Yes whatcanIgetyou?
Smile hi to Denver grinding another batch of beans;
Yes thank you six eighty-one please.
Someone will have to get that man's
papers off the table,

and do I need to brew another batch I forget.
Good morning what can I get you?; three people add
    themselves to the line—I
was waking up
in a tent
with Alec
two weeks ago this minute.
It was cold
we had a sleeping bag—
so divebackdownunder warm.
He was at the Lake House last night
while I stayed home,
having to get up at six for this,
and I wonder
when we will ever
wake up together
again?

Subservient

Janayah is actually smiling
and Denver cracking me up
each time
I go in the back.
No orders mixed up—
and I'm giving the right change.

I'm beginning to be used to it—
beginning to fit,
when in strides Iris-Casey-Josey-Miette.
Their eyes say *we know you,*
but their nostrils jerk like horses'
and their lips smirk, *we don't want to.*
Being almost cool here flushes suddenly into being hot
with embarrassment:
this stained apron,
my lank ponytail,
the empty wallet
I am hourly trying to fill.
Their cashmere scarves,
perfumed bangs,
the sheaves of cash flicked in manicured hands.

Skinny mochas, all of them
—*hold the whipped cream*—
and for the first time
all day
Janayah has to take over.
She's so angry
she makes me clean the espresso machine,
but at least the steam hissing
covers up their high laughs.
When they're gone I get the bussing bin,
and I think of Cinderella:
even after the glory of the ball she was
still wiping up after the stepsisters
—still on her knees
cleaning up their mess—
remembering the prince
and his quiet, handsome charm,
wondering if he'd already
forgotten
about her.

Covert Operation

Two minutes stolen Monday
in the far-left stall of the bathroom—me and my
   forbidden keypad—
saying simply that I love him,
risking everything for those words,
risking confiscation,
detention to remind him
that small
(gigantic) thing.

Busy Work

Afternoon of would-be no-work freedom
with my ankles chained instead
to scrubbing the bathtub,
vaccuming the foyer,
folding sheets and towels,
putting away each dish.
My housechores have piled up
clogging the table—cluttering the floor.
Mom pulls her weight, nursing at the hospital,
but she has me to do the cooking,
and no homework, either.
The acid unfurls now
across the back of my brain—
another afternoon without Alec,
another assignment in the way.

Why Poets Don't Belong
in the Marketing Department

The universe of literary thought
—and all of poetic genius—
perches
on its toenails this afternoon
clutching
at its own tunic
with consternation
and suspense.
Rama puffs,
Sara sighs,
Caitlyn dutifully
takes notes
as the debate of the ages—or at least the hour—
rages
through the silence
of barely-suppressed disdain.
Three calls for submissions face the judges:
—Mr. Burland insists, *choose today*—
one of Rama's
one of Sara's
—the best one Charlie's—

all not quite right.
Will the dyslexic cats
call forth good poetry?
Or the blacked-in butterflies
and Yorick skull?
Is an open coffin
festooned with roses
the current equivalent
of *I Want You*?
I wonder what Alec
would say
if he were here.
The ancients suck in their breath—
they are too stunned
—we are all stunned—
by our stupidity
to even speak.

On the Seventh Day

Holy Wednesday again and I am
supine in the cathedral of Alec's embrace.
Peace washes over his
loosening Adonis face and normally
I would let my eyes worship
for an hour
the pew-straight line of his nose and
the tender dip—Aphrodite's fingerprint—
of his upper lip
before moving
fully
to the praise of his mouth.
But today I am a child in church
swinging my feet and squirming,
glancing at the clock.
There is dinner, as always, to make for Mom
but also math homework undone,
a senior "exit survey" to complete for guidance,
call for submissions rewrites,
and a chemistry test
too close for comfort.
With work again Friday and

then on Saturday too
Sunday will be no day of repose,
the thought of which makes even this sanctuary
feel a little like work.
If God got a day of rest,
when will I?

Dramatic Shift

Face curled into my neck on the carpet, he says
Where are you? and I say *Where I always am:*
here.
And his strong arms are a band around me,
holding me in,
keeping me close.
No you're not. You're—
And I can't help it—*You think I'm where?—*
And then the arms are gone with the rest of him,
holding me
but somewhere else, somewhere I sent him:
some distant place full of worry and frown.
I'm right here—my hand on his arm—*it's just*
there's a lot . . .
And he really lets go.
You should probably go, I guess.
And I *should* probably go. I have
too much to do
to be here now.
But now I don't want to.
No I can stay. You just know how Mom is.
Dinner, you know.

And it is too long a pause,
it is too much space,
before he says, *Yeah. I know.*
I have nothing to say,
so I reach for my shirt.
It's just a phase, comes out of my mouth—
but they are just some words I read in a magazine,
some words I don't believe in,
words that
—by the face of him—
he doesn't believe either.

A Few of My Favorite Things

Adjusting the doughnuts in their tray:
single file,
curve to curve,
holes lined up like a string of pearls.

Finding that
the whole milk (or half and half, or skim milk) pitcher
is almost empty
and filling it
before anyone
knows it's needed.

Pulling down
out-of-date flyers
—tacked up by anyone—
from the congested bulletin board.

Walking in for my shift
after school,
Nadia
—all black spikes and dimply smile—
behind the counter, chirping,

Well what took you so long? and in general
being able to focus
on something else
for a change.

Thursday Night Latrine Duty

Someone has
spewed
in the women's bathroom—it is alloveritisreally a
mess
and Nadia needs me to clean it up; I say sure I have
four more tables to clear and then—.
Alec is
at the movies with Quinn-Blake-Steve and we
haven't texted in hours.
Maybe he is glad
that I am not there—maybe
I smell too much
like coffee and puke.

A Very (Un)Valentine
(with apologies to Gertrude Stein)

Very not-fine is my valentine
very not-fine and apparently not-mine.
Very not-mine is my valentine very not-wanting-to-
 be-mine and very not-fine.
Very not-fine is my valentine and not-mine,
very not-fine very
not-mine and not-(apparently)-mine is my valentine.

Valentine's Without You

Serving swooning couples all night long—
the wine and coffee poured
in scarlet-and-truffle streams for them,
their glasses glossed
with the sugar of sizzling smiles, but
my own chocolate center has filled up with poison,
the roses he gave me all twisted black.
He has decided to go out with friends
while I have to work,
covering for Nadia.
Tonight her woozy eyes will close in bliss,
her lips
part in succulent kisses, caressed,
while mine are clenched in all the things
I'm trying to say to him
but he won't hear—
too busy with everything he is doing without me,
(It's just a phase)
too surrounded by faces that are not mine—
those faux-friendly arms
twining themselves around him,
giving him something else

to focus on for a change.
My pillow is my only sodden comfort
until a bleary two AM—his silly sloshing voice
laughing,
trying to say he loves me,
wanting to know if he missed Valentine's.
My own voice chokes on anger he neither hears nor
understands.
Single girls weep today
but those of us in love
aren't supposed to be crying too.
Oh you stupid boy,
you have missed everything.

Camille

choosy

at the meat counter she points—not that chop but that one, not that filet but this. she is frown-lined and stern, difficult to wait on, difficult to understand. she pinches her purchases to her dragged-down bosom, clutches her keepsakes in her shawl. other people at the farmer's market move around her, avoid her disapproving glance, roll their eyes at the time she takes with her pointing, her assessing, her careful choosing. this sunday between mom and dad, clutching your own cardigan around your chest, frowning into yourself, you see her and pause. because you recognize her reasoning; there is a fraternity between you. she is careful. she is cautious. she is choosy and a critical judge. she will not take the imperfect meat. she will not bring the wrong one home.

empty calories

you certainly didn't think it was going to be edgar. sure, the
boys had all been jostling themselves in your direction for the
last couple of days, elbowing you unnecessarily, their laughter
always too loud and too desperate—their eyes sneaking to see if
you can see how clever they are, how much fun they're having,
how much fun you'd have if you were with them. but you were
figuring it'd end up being maybe simon or sam: one of the taller
boys who at least has a sense of style. but no it was edgar you
apparently swam up to on saturday (he made you laugh, you
knew he was kind) and now it is edgar again here after fourth
period, suddenly outside math class, wanting to see what's up,
wanting to know what's going on after school. *we could get
milkshakes*, he says, his earnest face going full-collapse when you
snark something about it not being 1952. *or just walk around
little five*, he corrects quickly, hunching his three-foot-wide
shoulders over his five-foot-four frame. you are all about starting
your next sentence with a stern, *look*, but then dorie passes by
with a big confusing thumbs-up and all you can hear is the swim
of bees. suddenly somehow it's after school and you are meeting
him on the quad and no one is looking but everyone sees you,
and it doesn't matter how casual they act with themselves and
each other, they're all so very *serious*, and for a minute you

picture yourself turning around, walking away, saying never mind, but you are still the new girl, you still need your friends, so you lift your chin and make yourself smile and this is so boring already but there you are, walking toward him, letting his hand find the small of your back.

different types of alone

he drives like your grandpa jared used to: gunning up behind the cars in front of him and hanging there so close and so tight that you can't help but grab on to the door handle and press your foot to the floor. you are not sure what the big hurry is especially since the traffic stays at each light for twelve minutes and you are only a few blocks away. you consider jumping out at ponce and moreland, telling him you forgot something, telling him you have to be home, but then the light changes and he guns through it—tailing—and you grit your teeth and try to think whether you'll want nachos or else just a smoothie. when you finally arrive he parks too close to the car next to you and you have to squeeze yourself out like an octopus between. he is waiting for you—but not really—by the sidewalk, eager to get there—wherever you're going—and as he crosses the street you watch him not even looking to see if you're there, but you follow anyway just to see what's next. he does not offer you a soda does not offer anything just walks straight into criminal and heads for the comics. you watch him awhile: head down, fingers flipping—he doesn't look up for you, doesn't know where you are. and you understand that he might really like you, but is one of those guys who really only wants the kind of company that will follow him around while he does things he'd do anyway, on his own, just so he doesn't have to look like he's alone. and while his independence is part of what made you kiss him at the lake house in the first place, you aren't that kind of lonely and there's plenty you could do alone yourself, so after flipping through some cds and buying a copy of *flaunt* you pat edgar on the back and tell him thanks but you're walking home. his face is a surprise-letdown swirl but you don't give him time to recover; you just half-wave and say thanks again. you don't walk home either—you go down to el myr instead and order a big plate of cheesy nachos and you sit there and read your magazine—glad to (really) be by yourself.

keep moving

you're all geared up for it to be maybe weird with edgar in the morning, but when you get to school you find his arm draped around some girl named holly. some girl from volleyball. some girl even ellen hardly knows; some girl you've never seen. and there's willow shooting her eyes at you and you trying to ignore them and edgar smiling like he just won musical chairs and you really just glad for that to be the end of it, but having to act a little miffed—having to give them something—just so they can leave you alone and let you go on with things, let you march with your drum in your own little private parade, because remember all you're doing is twirling your baton until you get to the end of the line. maybe it stings that he wasted no time, but he is a bee just like the rest of them and if he's found someplace to suck nectar you're glad it's not you who has to give him the buzz. you can already hear luli laughing about it anyway, wondering why you agreed to hang out with him in the first place. the goal is to keep yourself moving, remember? don't linger. don't hover. you are not going to stay.

things to miss about chicago #5

the el on a rainy day. stark skies. lakebeachwalking when it's way too cold. palmer house lobby. descartes coffee. needing a scarf. english class. that crazy kid in AP history with the weird slanting hair. sidewalk hot dogs. pigeons lifting up together. walking everywhere and anywhere. candace's small shoes next to your clodhoppers. sidewalks full of tulips. waving to boat-tour tourists from the bridge. feeling enclosed. feeling safe. art institute lions. the whorl of dark hair on the back of his neck. those hands that—

bridges

the trick about bridges is that—while they do span great distances: connecting two points that would ordinarily remain disconnected—if there's too wide a gap between their supports, the middle will sag and eventually break. even just a weak link will make the whole thing collapse. so bridges between things take time. you have to work from both sides. they require whole teams to design and construct. they take attention to detail, take great effort. and too many people are used to being islands, moored (isolated) in their own blue coconut seas of bliss, so it is harder and harder to find those who will build (who will believe in) bridges to anywhere else. you cannot make a bridge by yourself. there has to be someone working from the other end. and it is such a great distance. there is always, after all, so much (so much) water.

the coffeehouse

in charlotte it was starbucks, but that's only because it was
two blocks from school and everyone went there and you were
only thirteen, anyway. in sf you migrated to peet's which wasn't
much better but you weren't allowed to go all the way over
to vesuvio's, where you wanted to hang (even though they'd
never let you in). chicago was intelligentsia, where you really
developed your taste. special roast coffees, nonautomated
espressos, counter people who wore their own clothes, music
that wasn't chosen by some corporate office three states away,
but it was ruby's that taught you about cake—real cake inches
high and made by someone who likes it almost as much as you
do. since the atlanta arrival you've been looking for it—your
place, your hangout, your relaxing room, your coffee haven,
your kingdom of confection . . . and today you find it. today,
after school, tagging along into decatur behind ellen-jessica-
flip-simon-willow, you catch a glimpse and take note of the
friendly outdoor patio and the beckoning chalkboard with the
dancing monkey and the grinning goat. the aroma wafting out
the opened front door makes your toes curl with anticipation,
but you make yourself wait until later. later, when you're alone,
you'll slip into it like a much-needed bath.

by the bonfire

since it isn't raining this saturday there's a bonfire at the lake
house, and of course that means there's some asshole who
steps in it and melts half his shoe. there are girls with beers
in red cups standing stupidly close to the flames, coughing
and shifting away from the smoke, too dumb to step back, or
maybe afraid they'll squash the couples sitting cross-legged
together in the dark hem just outside the firelight's circle—
sounds of their make-outs audible even over everyone else
talking and the sharp crackle of spark. there's the helpful guy
in the life is good t-shirt who knows just when to put the next
log on—always ready with a big stick to poke things in place
when they collapse. you are enjoying the orange on your face,
the warm laughing banter around you, and tomorrow you will
bury your nose in your sweater, relish the way everything still
smells like camping.

more than meets the eye

and then suddenly you've got company. you knew when you saw
him last time—everyone in the whole pot-fogged, beer-goggled
house knew—that he was pretty much the hottest boy there—and
now here he is, hesitating a little, his shoulders unsure, but very
clearly standing next to you, watching the fire too. you remind
yourself girls will be like baseballs to him: catch, caress, throw
back out to the field. but when his eyes catch yours—catch
your eyes sneaking over to him—somehow the scales tip and
the fire brightens. or perhaps it dims. something in those eyes
surprises you for a second time, gives you a little pause. the most
popular boy by the lake and he looks genuinely lonely. you are
blushing—or too warm—and give him a small smile, but start
to step away (you have to keep moving). when he speaks at first
you don't quite understand. you think he is kidding. you think
he is making fun of you. you think you had him right in the
first place, but when you challenge his eyes with yours there's
no smirk, no asshole a-ha, and he says it again: *you seem you
could use / a little kind of surprise / maybe some haiku?* then just
stands there, open and waiting, while you count imperceptibly
on your fingers. he waits for you to do the math, for your eyes to
widen, for you to say, *in fact i do.*

Becca

Some Advice

When you are
wrung out like the dish towel
you had stuck in your shorts all day
instead of an apron,
and your hair is still wet
from the shower you needed
in order to rinse off all that coffeegrime and sweat
—when you still have to read
three chapters for English
one chapter for history
and have not studied for that chemistry test—
do not be surprised if,
when you go to the party (late) anyway
to try to lean on your boyfriend
and laugh at Paul's jokes,
you find yourself rolling your eyes at everyone and
more than once squeezing your temples from noise.
Try to feel no shock either when
Alec scowls because you won't
do chickenfights by the bonfire,
or when he says, *What's the matter with you?*

in that cold way you hate
and you find yourself leaving
—too early—
in tears.

Showing, Not Telling: To Alec

Your surprise
is a surprise.
How could you think
—*What are you thinking?*—
I could possibly act
—*I don't understand*
why you're acting this way—
like a girl going through normal
—*I need you to be normal*—
when there's no more routine,
and this distance
—*It's not such a big deal*—
is a dance that divides us,
a daily departure
—*We still talk every day*—
from all I know how to do.
Did you really think
—*How can you think that?*—
after this morning's phone call
—*I have to go, Becca. You have to be cool.*—
I could be anything but uncool:
wouldn't show up on your doorstep,

—What are you doing here?—
shout *surprise*
in your face
until you stop blinking—
until you listen to me
—Listen, Becca—
till you finally *see?*

Failed Advice

Mom doesn't like it when I slam the door,
shut her out,
say I'm not hungry enough for dinner.
She comes in anyway,
sits
on the edge of my bed, says,
Just try to project yourself into tomorrow
when you've calmed down and everything's fine.
She doesn't understand
—it never got fine with her and Dad—
that time without him is the opposite of fine,
and every tomorrow he's not in
isn't one I want
to be projected into.

Gross Dividends

The highest commodity in econ class is laughter
and indifference
dressed in khaki pants and cocky guffaws.
No one cares about anything
but proving how little they care
as Mrs. Marchpane vaults herself somehow
—who got her here?—
into a discussion of Victoria's Secret underwear.
It's like a science, a social experiment, seeing who
can derail her faster
onto a wilder track of conversation,
the popular boys—
one-two-three in a row: so handsome
and so cruel—all lobbing
softballs of distraction at her which she
catches in both hands, showing off for them.
We're supposed to be learning
about the mechanics of the world:
bonds, dividends, supply and demand.
I don't want to be learning these things—
I don't need them—
and this waste-of-time class
sucks out my already-aching soul.

Do-Over

I should be
writing strings of apologies, composing
pages of *forgive me* sonnets that would shame
both Neruda and Keats.
I should be
knocking on his door again,
taking back the things I said,
wrapping
my arms, my brain, my heart, my life
around him and promising
to never let him go, but
Tuesday afternoon and
this second chance in writer's forum
won't come our way again.
I have to be strong. I have to be a leader.
Indecision
has wracked us for a week,
but Mr. Burland
has pitied,
giving us more time.
Time to lick our wounded egos
time to put our heads together
time to correct

the mistakes (of our editorial) past.
Like me and Alec,
none of us can agree
but we all agree
last year was a disaster
and we don't want to duplicate
the sorry magazine
no one bought last year.
In this we are united.
In this we have some hope.
In this we have the strength
to work together
make a mash-up masterpiece
that makes us proud.
Let my colleagues inspire me
into reunification, connection, restoration.
Collaboration, smile upon us;
humility crown our heads.
Creativity bring your blessing;
pride you have no place here
until we are finished, and victorious.
Until we are over this and done,
until I can call him, proud.

How to Make the World a Better Place, One Poster at a Time

Stretch the hour along your arm.
Track its progress
—its slow-then-speeding bend
across the afternoon:
twisting itself from
a crowd of cumulonimbus to
a rainbow of success beaming
across everyone's faces.
Bring together
four jaded seniors all scuffed
and scarred
from last year's magazine disaster and blow into them
a little more disbelief,
a little more despair.
Let them scowl. Do not fear. They will
soon exhaust themselves with
their own soured sighs.
Grant them mercy.
Allow a new poster suggestion
from two timid sophomores
to slide across the table and sit

in the seniors' laps.
Let them remember
being unlistened to last year—let them
recognize
gold when it's struck.
Combine
their expertise and
a little cunning—let them
listen, question, improve.
Notice
even the teacher is smiling, see
what pure collaboration can do.
At the end of the hour find
eight children skipping
down the hallways together—
believe
that a common passion
can make anything possible.

Inspired

I shouldn't be texting
in my (only recently repaired) car, but
it is mostly at a stop sign and
there are never any cops on this stretch.
You are the flint. I am the fire, I type,
Fanning it only makes it burn stronger.
Without much thought I press—vigorously—send.
He is probably in practice, but
I am today full of oxygen,
am stoked high on kindling,
and he helps me breathe.

Bad Timing

Break time at work
and at the end of this awful week,
I want to keep things light with us
—only tenderly repaired—
just tell him
what Nadia said
about two forks and a rusty knife.
Now two rings,
three,
and his voice is late-night distracted
flung out the passenger window
of a speeding car.
My lungs are constricting. I am going numb.
Just tell me how much you love me
bubbles weakly from my mouth.
I'm a nuisance.
An inconvenience.
A bother,
getting in the way.
I do. He insists. *But I've got to go.*
It's not such a big deal. It's all okay.
And then it's just me,

on the patio,
a muted phone in my hand
two hours left of work and
the helium balloon of my heart,
deflating
rapidly.

Disappearing Pennies

Nickels, dimes, quarters where
do these whole dollars go,
betraying me at the end of my shift—
time to count the drawer?
Two-sixteen under.
Five twenty-nine over.
Sixty-three cents short.
Night after night,
bleary-eyed, swollen-ankled and I am
sweeping change into my hand and back again
counting over and over
praying to the calculator gods,
Please make this add up right.
The spool of paper rolls out,
the purple numbers spinning and I am
four ninety-one over
one seventy-six short.
Margot notes it down in her yellow pad
—it will come out of my check
even the overage—
her eyebrow arcing high with disapproval
and impatience,

my hands open with apologies she won't hear.
I am not sure where the mistakes come from,
how my fingers manage
to slip and miss—
even worse, how they swim together each day,
adding me up to one fat zero.

If I Go

Everyone is already at the Lake House,
including him.
Midnight, and I am
sweaty, stained, and in slow motion.
I could
go home and shower, dress, make-up
and get myself ready
—make it to the party by two—
maybe enough time
for a sloppy kiss,
a covert make-out,
or another misunderstanding—
another slammed door.
I could also
go home and shower, pajamas, DVD
curl up in bed and maybe
swap a foot massage with mom.
Would he love me more
if I went?
Or if I knew better
and stayed?
Pulled in so many directions

I am too tired
—too ground and gritted—
to care
either way.

Camille

girl's best friend

when it's wet and cold and raining all day like this and the ground is soppy-gross with dead leaves and runny clay you can't take the dogs outside all together to run around in their big playground pen out back. instead they get small group rotations for a bit in the back room—the one full of dog toys and an observation window, the one that smells too much like pee. it is not supposed to feel like a jail in there but it does at least to you, so when you and the puppies are there playing you do your best to clap your hands and chase and tug on things that they clamp in their mouths—roll around with them and wrestle and keep your voice high and cheery. because while you do have your own bathroom and come and go as you please, you know what it is like to be somewhere you don't want to be. you know all about being pent up and stuck. you know how nice it is to have even a stranger come in and let you run around with them, pretend you aren't trapped inside even if they can't take you home. it's still nice to have someone who will let you lick their face.

casing the joint

still cold nasty san fran winter-style raining outside: not a
downpour or a gusty gale or hail or sleet—just a slow steady
curtain of wet that makes everything bone-achy and shivery,
even though it's not that cold. you drive yourself around in a
couple of circles between the shelter and downtown decatur,
going the wrong way at the courthouse, finding a dead end
where you didn't expect one, squinting through the windshield.
but finally you find the goat-monkey place again and even
more miraculously manage to wrangle a parallel parking
spot right out front. to you it seems like perfect coffeehouse
weather but maybe everyone is cozed up at home with their
gas fireplaces and their nubbly sweaters, because when you
walk in—moving quickly, keeping in a straight line, acting
like you've been here plenty of times before, this takes no
thought—there's only a snuggly couple together on one of
the couches and three individuals all ghost-lit by whatever's
beaming through their laptop screens. you order what you
always order, because there's never any kind of stupid coffee
code for it, no sizes to guess or syrups to memorize: decaf
and cake—the first cake that catches your eye, the chocolate
raspberry mousse one that says it's vegan though you could
care less. when you sit you can finally really look around:
cool black-and-white photos (or paintings made to look like

black-and-white photos) on the wall—on closer inspection, by a local artist—warm wood floors with assorted worn rugs underneath. small tables with things painted on the tops surrounded by chairs straight from a parisian café. deep leather armchairs and small, well-placed halogen lights on thin wires from the exposed-beam ceiling. you feel yourself let out your breath, settle in. you take a sip of the rich creamy coffee, a bite of chocolate soft explosion. this will do. it will do indeed.

afterimages

days later and you still feel like you had double vision all of
saturday night, watching that big baseball facade with the sad
soft inner core shining out through those brown eyes. usually
people are all they are, wearing themselves on their sleeves (even
if they're hiding something) but this was a double-exposed
photograph in the flesh, flashing back and forth. for all that
muscle he didn't try anything—didn't even allude to it—and
that was at least noticeable if not refreshing. you were just two
people—a boy and a girl—standing by a fire, swapping small
talk, laughing at the goofs around you, just standing there
watching the flames in silence. and for a girl who's got to stay
in motion it surprised you how it was nice for a while, just
being able to stand still. which is maybe why you gave him your
e-mail, there at the end. maybe you thought he wouldn't write.
sure, maybe that's it. but you can still feel the heat of that fire
now, the peace and quiet of him next to you, reading this new
inbox message: *peacock girl who hides / treasure maps of mystery: /
a camouflage smile.* you have the impression he's trying to make
an impression, but you've lost count of whether it's first, second,
or third. you're too preoccupied counting out syllables over and
over. counting the syllables—finding them exactly right.

luli's laugh

you call and tell her about the catcher. and at first she laughs
and you think she (like you) is just amused by it all—a baseball
player writing poetry, how ludicrous—but then her voice turns
serious and she says *you're not really serious, are you?* and you
say, *what?* and you don't mean for it to be so defensive, don't
mean to sound as though you're protecting anything, but then
she laughs again and says *i get it; never mind.* and you insist, *no
really, what?* and she says you're a funny girl. and asks have you
gotten any good mail lately. and you don't know what kind of
mail she means (mailbox or inbox), and you don't think she'll
be able to listen to either kind, with that judging laugh, even
though she's a fan of chicago and might want to know, so you
keep it all to yourself and change the subject. you tell her a
joke about the girls at school. you give her something to really
laugh about.

speaking from experience

you can still hear luli laughing over it but the truth is you just can't stop thinking about that catcher with the haiku. you're not really sure why and half the time you think even thinking about him might in some way be swimming against the wrong current. when it comes down to brass tacks all you really have is yourself. why pretend there's ever anything other than that? why can't that be *okay*? what are you going to do with that boy in chicago—go through the whole darcy thing again, go back to writing and writing—trading photos every day so she could see your new town, so you could still see your old one—until marissa kept showing up in her photos and then those photos became fewer and fewer while yours kept coming, trying to prove how cool life was in charlotte—even though it wasn't. are you going to do that with every new connection you make, in every new town? yes those chicago postcards and the memories attached to them are lovely (and wouldn't it be so nice if you could have him every day—if we could—), but people don't get to keep anything forever so who are you kidding? sure luli would say, *well how do you know?* she says spending your life trying not to get hurt is not really living, that she wants to live like a trapeze artist: if her body tells her to jump she does it because otherwise she'd just be cowering there on the platform when she could be flying and leaping with someone, maybe even for a long time. that's what luli thinks. but everyone loves luli. luli's never had letters unanswered. she's never sent photos no one wants to see.

not getting ready for a date

it's not like it's a date. how could it be a date since you don't date anyone, because dating's a trap, because dating is totally dated? because you are the girl who stays unconnected to everyone. still, you do know he will be at the lake house tonight. and he knows you will be there. and you both know that right now you are probably getting ready to be there, knowing the other one will be there. it's why you're sitting here staring at your closet with a disaster of discarded outfits on your floor. it's why you can't decide between jeans or the deconstructed tuxedo pants. it's why you wish you'd bought those killer turquoise cowboy boots you saw with mom last weekend, and why you can't decide if your hair goes down or up. he'll be there. you'll be there. and eventually you'll be there together. and you're not sure what's going to happen—what's already happened is confusing enough—but you do know you're sure something will happen. maybe like last time you'll just talk. but that was still something. something for sure. he thought it was something too because what about those e-mails? so this isn't just going to another weekly party. it's more like kind of a date. even though you don't date. which is why you're not sure why you're sitting here getting ready as though it is a date. but why you're not able to act like it isn't one, either.

the kiss

he just comes at you. you barely drop much of a *hey, how are you?* there on the back deck where people can see—and he just comes *at* you, surprising as a tornado on a sunny day, blowing the roof off, pulling up the fence. you see him and you smile and then it's just one step, two steps and he's over you and under you and all over you and it's not some *you're cute i might like you* kiss, nor a confused and disgusting sloppy-slather fueled by all that vodka kool-aid he's obviously had. no, this is a mouth with momentum, a train on one track paying no heed to any warning clangs, a chemistry set just waiting for someone to put the wrong powder in the right tube and make something explode. this kiss says he needs you more than all those puppies put together, that he'll aim over and over at the tender haiku buried deep in your own trenches until he hits the right syllable. this kiss will wipe your mind of all things, will make you forget your name your face what town you're living in and who's driving you home. it is a kiss that, when it ends—after he's summoned laughing into the dark by shouting boys in the driveway—will leave you gasping and glossy-eyed for hours later, will follow you home as you stare in the bathroom mirror at the chewed-looking spots his stubble left on your chin. it is a kiss so loud and long that your whole mind will scream, *that can't happen again,* while your body will still twitch a little, wondering if it could just once more.

memory reset

monday lunch and ellen is all eyes and ears wanting to know about you and the catcher, the boy you forced yourself to forget all day yesterday, doing french extra credit you don't need, making sure your mind didn't wander—helping mom with dinner, organizing your socks. now ellen is nudging and winking so loud that dorie and willow and autumn and connor and even some of the boys are curious, looking at you, listening in. when you try to brush her off with rolling eyes and a flick of the wrist ellen says *oh no* and grabs your shoulders and presses her forehead against yours and says in this silly deep voice *you were having an illicit mind-meld and we want to know all about it.* and you laugh a little and think *was that it?* some kind of meeting-of-the-minds that's resulted in yours now being a little half-melted when you think about him? maybe you need to remind yourself that a clash of personality traits you didn't first anticipate does not—does not—mean the world's reversed its poles, that you don't still know exactly how this is all going to wind up in a few short months anyway, no matter how many haiku he writes or how he kisses. even these friends now—look at them, look at their faces closely—will be gone and leave you, and you will leave them, and you know that. wrap your arms around their shoulders now, drive in their cars to parties, pinky swear you've never met anyone like them before, have your slumber parties and hold them close, but remember the thing you know and they don't is that this time right now is even more fleeting than you think. remember all you are doing— with anyone—is killing time. (though killing time with a catcher who can kiss like that seems a lot nicer than killing time alone.)

Becca

New Morning

Force myself
to get up at five AM—master
the half-blind hair wash,
the sticky-eyed climb
into clothes I don't care about.
Suffer silent
along the empty-blue-black drive
past houses with their hats
still over their eyes,
the trees waiting in dark quiet
for the golden tickle
that means the sun.
Straighten my spine
on the crisp-cold walk
to the back bakery door
with its warm yellow light.
Inside inhale
deep enough to make my toes uncurl:
coffee-cinnamon-pastry-welcome
—a new morning
no one else has smelled.
Work quickly,

filling glass cases with
warm pumpkin-buttery bundles,
croissant toasty crispness
and deep doughnut delish.
Laugh with Nadia
—her smile
always on anyone,
but this morning, just me.
Clasp
the steaming mug
offered in my direction.
Realize
how much I like it—
starting the day this way.

Telephone Evolution

In the old days (Mom says)
it would just ring and ring and ring,
callers counting
twenty, twenty-one, (he could be
just now running in from outside)
before giving up.
Next came answering machines
(we still have an ancient one for the telemarketers)
that allowed for screening—
deciding whether or not
to pretend to be out.
Now there is the cell phone:
more immediate, less discreet—
I can tell, for example, after two rings and a click
that for the first time
he has seen my number, hit IGNORE.

The Coffee (Heart) Break

After the superspeedway
of Sunday morning doughnut drive,
coffee chaos,
and tablewipe tumbling
there is a small lull
—a pause.
I can sip
my own coffee—break
my own doughnut into small pieces to savor.
This is the time
—Freya knows—
someone can come by
and I can do more
than wave at her like a drowned girl.
She can come
—fifteen minutes before the after-church lunchers—
and I can sit
on the patio with her a minute,
ask about last night.
It is enough time even
for her to show me her phone

—the photos she took last night at the Lake House—
and ruin my life
forever.

With Apologies to WCW

so much depends upon
the red (handed) cameraphone photo
glazed with pain
(of him) standing beside
(with his mouth all over)
the (creamy) white chick

Numb

At first a column of heat
—a lava charge—
bursts up from the tail end of my spine and
rockets
up to the top of my skull
—fills my eyes—
so that for a moment I can't see and all I feel is
heat.

But it is the last thing I will feel—this fever wind—
because after that I am ice:
a white tundra of unmoving blank:
a glacier only very slightly drifting
—unaware of its own motion—
across a dark and frozen sea.

Fury

Freya's face is a fist,
her frustration a force
unfurled and frenzied—lashing
against the redhead, my boyfriend,
the entire (cheating) world.

Coming from her each hate-filled word falls—
one poisonously sour grape after the next,
leaving a miserable, permanent stain
on everything touched.

Island of Relief

After Freya leaves, the sorrow is a tidal wave,
pounding me so hard it is difficult to see
—strident tide smashing
everything in sight.

I am a drowned girl:
lungs grabbing dark water,
filling with—[seeking]—the source that will
silence and bury.

A pale hand plunges—grabs—
and insists: rise.
I am a gasping, sputtering face,
looking for a life raft.

Nadia is calm, cool, solid—
an ivory island.
In her comforting concern I will rest and think,
gulp for air,
try to breathe again.

Helpful Advice

Janayah's left alone at the counter
and I will get in trouble,
but I don't care I
can't breathe after all.
Back in the kitchen Nadia
holds me by the scruff of the neck,
helping me stand,
cleaning me up.
I know it hurts, Nadia says calmly,
but if he cheats, it's over.
Maybe not over for you
but over for him
and in that case it is just
over for you both.
Over like the last pizza crust.
Over like hitting E with forty miles
to the next fill-up.
Over like a blackout.
Over like an execution.
Her face is still a new doll to me—something
to admire but not yet fully know.
But her voice is serious as the grave:

concrete, set and poured.
Break it off, she tells me,
sounding like some Old Testament Bible verse
about a right hand and its offense.
You have no choice, she says.
This girl usually so full of sunshine,
now black clouds sweep across her brow.
Against her finality my heart thuds, once.
But around it my soul echoes empty,
her words careening back and forth and back,
ringing like truths.

And Yet the Boss Wants Me to Smile

My body is
scarecrow scraps of hay held together
by unshed tears.
My voice
a strangled crackle
squeezed between imprisoned cries
scratching my throat.
The afternoon clock mocks
—each slow second a shard lodged in skin.
How can I ring up coffee
as though it is important,
when I can't imagine anything
being important
again?

Recipe for a Confrontation

Begin with
one hideous rumor,
two awful photographs,
and three cups of doubt.

Stir in
a difficulty nearly a whole week long
and five phone calls today
unreturned in a row.
Throw in three dashes of insecurity,
or more, to taste.
Bring all this to a boil and then simmer,
watching for the rime of bitter salts
that will accumulate along the edge.

When everything is the consistency
of hard, suppressed tears,
add, finally, his actual answering the phone,
and one long—very long—and awkward pause.
Gently combine an accusation,
and three demands for an explanation.

Wait for him to say something.
And wait some more.

Your crust will begin to brown,
but do not open the oven too soon.
Listen
for the escape of steam from him
—it will sound like a sigh—
and his hesitant gurgle, *Well* . . .

Only when everything
is burnt beyond denial,
and his explanations have boiled away, leaving
half-baked apologies you don't believe
will you know
for sure
that you are done.

Words I Never Thought I'd Say

I'm finished with you.
Don't call me.
I can't believe you.
I hate you.
Don't call me—*ever*.
How could you—how could you.
You are nothing special, and
I don't believe in you—never did.
You are just like the rest of them.
You are *just like* the rest of them.
You are just like the rest of them.
You are dead to me.

Amputation

My arm's been lopped off.
There it is
on the floor
not bleeding anymore but still
bloody.
It is an odd thing
—cold—
to look down and see a part of you
there,
but not where it's supposed to be.

I look around my room,
see proof of
what it was to have two arms:
photos
of both entwined around another;
pillows
held closely in sleep;
scissors, pencils, dirty forks
once deftly used with the now-gone hand;
my closet full of
shirts with two sleeves.

It hurts too much not to have it;
phantom pains.
I pick up the knife
—I will figure out how to use it right—
begin cutting away at my heart.

Falling on Deaf Ears

Only a hour after
ending everything, my phone rings and it is
Alec's number on the screen.
All the things he might say,
all the things I want him to say,
all the things he can't possibly say I
don't want to say anything:
press my phone
off.

Surreality

Walking through a misting fog
of bleakness all afternoon:
somehow my body has moved itself
from here
to here
—sleepwalking.
A terrible dream
only finally made real
when Mom's home-from-work hug surrounds me,
asking,
How was your day?

Camille

everyone is suddenly a lesbian

it must've been reading all that gertrude stein, or the special
focus on women's history month, but innocent wednesday
morning, and who suddenly made everyone a lesbian? first
connor and autumn, apparently no longer just best friends but
now hanging off each other and letting the sides of their hands
grace the sides of their boobs so that everyone on the sidelines
can see. then dorie admits loudly that she feels cold-shower
funny every time she sees zooey deschanel in a magazine. next
ellen—yes, ellen!—at lunch checks out daphne with different
eyes, and when you get to your coffeehouse there are two girls
tonguing each other on the front couch plain as day. you are
trying to be cool about it—what do you care; you lived in san
francisco you love lesbians you're sure your cousin is one—but
today you can't help but wonder with the sky so low and the
humidity getting turned up, the baseball players suddenly
leaving the field empty just like your inbox—you wonder if the
cosmos isn't just screaming for you to turn sappholesbo too.

mystery mail #3

it takes four days after its arrival for you to finally look at it:
lacy victorian thing showing a gray furry kitten wearing a pink
satin bow. someone has sprayed it with rose perfume. *where are
you, kitten?* in green pen is the only thing scrawled on the back.
you know without looking—the postmark's from chicago.

unwanted memory #3: first date

it was one of your only real dates—not like those afternoons
when you hung around the art institute waiting for his shift
to end so you could walk around together, or when he simply
managed to "run in to you" while you read and did homework
at ruby's after school. for this one he took the elevator and rang
your doorbell. for this one he had flowers. you weren't sure if
it was weird for him to meet your parents, or if that's what was
supposed to happen. you hadn't really had boyfriends before—
only boys—and weren't sure you wanted one—only wanted
him—so you had to just take your cues from him, from mom
and dad. you had your hair down for once. you were wearing
a dress. and sure when you came into the living room, when
your mom lifted her smile to you like that, you felt a little like
there should be a live studio audience breaking into applause.
but he shook hands with your father and you knew you'd never
seen someone more handsome. you were blushing all over your
body and you noted to yourself even then how you could feel
the glow of your heart moving at the edges of your skin. it
was scary and it was wonderful and he took your hand right
in front of them and you followed him down the hall. how it
turned into this you couldn't remember—him talking to you,
you talking to him—it simply turned and there you were,
golden and falling. dinner. candles. his straight teeth. your

nervous giggle. when you got home mom had arranged the flowers he brought—lilies—in a vase and put them on your dresser. you lay on top of the covers still in your clothes. you put your hands over your swirling heart and inhaled deeply. you almost fainted from the dizzy perfume.

disappearing act

it's not like you'd established a pattern. but having someone
who was maybe really here in the same town as you had
definitely demonstrated its appeal. the catcher wrote you, you
thanked him, he sent you something funny, you sent him
something funny back. you wanted to keep it simple and light,
and that's what it was. you wanted to be able to just see where
it went, and that seemed to be how it was going. but then there
was that moment on the deck, that moment you went blind
and he was seeing for the both of you, guiding you to a place
you didn't want to go and yet weren't ready to turn back from,
where everything was deadly still and yet dizzily swirling at
the same time. and you felt like it was different, but it could
still be clean. so you thought by now he would say *something*
about it, but instead there's this weird dirty silence you don't
understand. you're trying not to care but find yourself caring—
checking your inbox, looking for footprints in the sand,
traces of presence, overturning stones where there's nothing
underneath. each time, nothing. and it brings a kind of crazy
feeling back in you, this feeling of searching. you feel your skin
crawling. you feel yourself starting to pace.

lopsided bowls

like you're in kindergarten or seventh grade, mom's picking you up after school and won't tell you where you're going. ellen's kicking around, waiting with you, wearing friday drifty eyes and smiling into the sunshine, so when mom arrives and ellen bounces up to her, suddenly it's a mommy-daughter-friend date and you're hoping mom's not going to embarrass you. ellen's chattering away like they're old pals and you are astonished how always-easy she is, like luli, this immediate affection between them and everyone else. you drive through decatur, past the farmer's market, turning down some side street with a bunch of warehouses and who-knows-where. she stops at mudfire and ellen squeals, *i love this place*, and your mom's smile is a daffodil, yellowing the both of you. inside there are flats of clay, unattended wheels, the smell of wet stone and a kind, small woman who's glad to see you all. ellen knows what she's doing, sets to work already, but you and mom need a tutorial, need some help. an hour later and your thigh is cramped your hands are gunked and you've got a lopsided bowl that would spill anything that you put inside. ellen's draped over mom's shoulder, guiding her hands, steering the clay, and they're both laughing and comfortable, working together. you see luli again superimposed over ellen, what better daughters they make for your so-eager mother: sisters of fun. their vases are tall and straight and perfect for peonies. yours still don't get it, are all still crumpled and squashed.

m.i.a.

another saturday night and you swim around for a while—
float, really—talking to ellen and some new boy eric, some
group of his friends, some kids from another private school
whose names you don't know but seem they'd be the kind
found on gravestones buried in the woods somewhere:
somewhere near a secret pool, with mossy rocks and shadows.
you are by the bonfire, you are back inside, you are hovering
near the keg, you are dancing with a boy with chocolate skin
whom you've never seen before now. you are not in a hurry
and you are not anxious (he is always here; he always is), until
it's after twelve thirty and you haven't seen him yet. you look
good—you made sure to even though he's said (how can he
have said) nothing—and even willow says so. one o'clock, one
thirty and you're moving in circles: foyer-hallway-dining room.
kitchen-living room-den. the back deck is empty now (he is
always here; he didn't say he wouldn't be here; how could he
not be here), the bonfire is dying, and you know people have
paired off and all the bedrooms are full. he didn't say he'd be
here, but he didn't say he wouldn't (he didn't say *any*thing),
and now you're getting self-conscious, are aware of the strain in
your neck. you are actively looking now, and you look stupid.
you are hanging too close to the front door. you are listening
for cars. you are watching for a boy who won't come.

provincial

three days cooped up in school-friend-home routine and you
want to be going somewhere, no matter where you're going.
while mom and dad are happycontentpleasedandsmiling with
the miraculously green lawns here—the vast space the quieter
neighborhoods—you feel like a tiger in a cage, pacing always
pacing. no matter how far you walk, where you're going is
nowhere. or at least nowhere you want to stay for very long.
there are the shops in va-hi there is piedmont park there are
places along ponce but after you've made those trips once
or twice there is no more to it and no interesting way back.
your feet-knees-ankles-elbows-brain all ache for the feeling
that no matter where you're going you're always going to
end up somewhere. even business blocks would have a new
coffeehouse or bookstore or little café you'd never seen before,
or at least a warehouse with some challenging graffiti. now
the restlessness is starting to define you—not just in your
brain but in your body, in your teeth. your atlanta friends
don't understand—they've used the same routes and seen the
same signs; they think moving two states is a big deal, think
trading hookups every other weekend is exotic. and you can't
blame them. they grew up here they know here this is home
to them—it's the way things should be. they don't understand
why, when there's a moving sidewalk at the airport, you will

always take it, because it means you will get to the next point that much faster—you will see the new thing first you will be there you will not be stuck behind anyone you will be moving; you will get ahead.

and there are couples like that everywhere

the puppies are tired of being cooped up too and with the
weather maybe-warming and the sky not as dark early, you ask
lily if it's okay to let all of them out a half hour longer. even
when she smiles she has that frown between her brows but you
are a hard worker and do things without being asked so she
agrees it's probably not a bad idea. everyone is happy-mouth-
tails-eyes once they get outside and you are chasing a few of
them near the back of the yard when lily comes out and you
think at first she's changed her mind, but then you see she
is with a young couple and they are heading straight for the
long-legged half-collie mutt girl with the patches of brown on
her slender face. lily has a leash and she clips one end to the
collar gives the other to the man (he is towering over his blond
wife—from here he looks eight feet tall) and the four of them
go inside and you know the papers they will be filling out, the
questions lily will be answering, and you watch the other dogs
playing and running as though nothing has happened and you
think to yourself, *huh. just like that.*

springing

back in chicago they're all hunched against slicing winds,
wearing layers of fleece and re-waterproofing their boots, while
you and mom are in shorts and t-shirts, light hoodie jackets,
heading over to the park to play a few rounds of tennis friday
after school. there are things starting to bud here, flowers
about to explode, and you have heard about the southland in
the springtime but you still are not fully prepared for this, still
find it odd when girls are wearing skirts to school. at the park
everyone has got the same idea—the first sunny weekend of the
season—even a few girls in bikini tops, sunning themselves on
towels. it will get cold again (you can feel it in the breeze)—
and people (boys) will still find a way to disappear—but for
now it is beautiful and brilliant. for now it feels good to open
the windows, to think a familiar face might round the corner
and smile at you, might leave a tulip on your front porch,
might stick around for a week. for now you are open to any
and all of it, for now you want to let the sun in, stretch your
muscles, empty your brain and air yourself out.

One Art
(with apologies to Elizabeth Bishop)

The art of losing is hard to master;
though others do seem filled with the intent
to be lost that their loss should be no disaster.

Lose someone every day. Accept the loneliness
of lost friends, the hour badly spent with another.
The art of losing is hard to master.

Then practice losing farther, losing faster:
acquaintances, and names, and where it was
you meant
to meet someone. All of these will bring disaster.

I lost my mother's trust. And look! my last, or
next-to-last, of three loved classmates went.
The art of losing is hard to master.

I lost two best friends, lovely ones. And, vaster,
some realms I owned, seven months—a true love.
I miss it. And it was a disaster.

—Especially losing him (the soothing poems, a chest
I love) I shan't have lied. It's evident
the art of losing's too hard to master
and I know it looks like a disaster.

Sensory Overload

He can't not
think of me I know he
does.
He must.
because I can't
hear
see
smell
feel
find
anything
that doesn't have
his name
his scent
his taste
his smile
his self
all over it.

Extinguished

Once a fire burned in me but now it is extinguished
    and I
cannot even catch the scent of smoke.
Ashes, ashes.
Only ashes.
It's been a week of darkness. A week of
nothing, I can't
even remember yesterday.
The artifacts of my disappearance: tissues
strewn across my floor, hair a tangled dirty mess,
jeans hanging on my hip bones
from seven days of being unable to eat.
There is no fire in here. The fire is gone.
I finally write these words—these sodden words—
because once I was a fire-maker, and I don't
know how
to do anything else.
But they are damp words, wet words,
and they will never catch.
Scratching with bits of charcoal,
my hands are black—blackened—
with these attempts.

Not even one coal left
to light a torch, illuminate
what has happened in the last week,
what will happen in the week ahead.
I am blind, scratching in ashes.
There is no fire.
And I am cold.

Message in a Bottle

Midnight? Sunset? I do not know
light from day or dark from darker.
These waves toss me
from room to room,
not really seeing and
tasting only salt.
I am floating on a gray sea, giving
my body to the sharks, my dead heart to the tide,
when a message swims up,
a foreign text in a cell phone bottle:
you are the one who
knows everything in my soul—
which is lost forever.
Heavy with crust my eyes swim gray.
There is nothing anymore I want to see;
these are the scratchings of a crazy man,
someone alone and moored
on an island where the trees bear only
fruits of humiliation
and deceit,
where strange birds call from trees,
and the natives eat
each other's hearts.

Gossip Fodder

Misty Monday gray outside:
weather for a zombie attack,
and perhaps they'd mistake me for their kind.
I stare
into my locker a long time before I can take
    anything out,
trying to visualize myself
making it through another week at all,
when Freya appears,
poking her bony bent knees in the backs
of my straight ones,
making my legs half drop out
from under me.
Laughing, her face is all mouth
with four slits for eyelids, nostrils.
The rest, freckles.
So many sometimes—I don't mean to—I wonder
what she got called
on the elementary school playground.
She's had a Blow-Pop for breakfast:
a big wad of pink gum snaps in her teeth
—the sugar cloud floating from her glossy lips—
and her tongue is green.

Just trying to make you laugh, she smacks,
grimacing a grin.
I feel miserable
and want to be left alone. I'm
not even sure why we're friends anymore,
where she came from,
why she's sticking around,
but I can't say any of that because now
—now that I abandoned
all my other friends for Alec—
she's pretty much all I've got.
Her voice turns serious: *He wasn't there.*
And I know where she means and when she means,
and I know who she means and I don't know
if I want to know this or not.
Probably a hot date, I snort. But she is ready for me.
No but she was. And looking for him, you could tell.
But trying not to.
I had
to hang out in the stoner garage I was so pissed,
seeing her there.
Her gum cracks and her gloss gleams. Her blue eyes
bore into mine. I can see
her nostrils working with excitement.
I don't want to listen to her,
but it is better than just
reading alone in the library,

better than being with no one. And maybe
if Freya spins it right, I can make believe
it really is just another bit of gossip,
and not something awful
happening
to me.

Being Hamlet

We're reading him out loud in class
and Mr. Burland is letting me
be the prince.
Dark days, dark mood,
dark-ness—
the dark of him enfolds me while I read,
and I am wrapped in his misery
instead of mine.
Oh unholy ghost
—oh twisting tempest—
how I too know the paralysis
of loss.
Reading, it's as though I *am* him:
so angry you could weep,
so sad you want to kill someone,
so confused you can do neither.
I read.
And when I am done everyone looks
as though an electric current
has passed through the room.
No one

will look squarely at me.
It is like I've been possessed
and they are afraid
this sorrowed ghost will climb into them too.

Bittersweet Victory

The call for submission posters we created
have done their job.
After school at writer's forum
and Mr. Burland is pleased, handing
two stacks of stories and poems over—already
a pile thick enough for a magazine,
with two weeks still to go
and more rolling in.
Some of these are good,
Sara says, grunting in her own surprise and
handing me a batch to see
for myself.
Even Rama is smiling,
looking over Caitlyn's shoulder, laughing
at a bad metaphor but
quite obviously tickled
by the bounty we've reaped
after such hard work.
We should be
tossing the papers up in the air, letting
these entries rain down on us like confetti.
We have

done better than last year and
our magazine
—from the initial looks of it—
might be
something
we would all actually read.
I should be happy.
I should be proud.
But I should also be able
to tell Alec
about this.

Sighting

Just after the rush of a was-busy Thursday
—people have cleared—and I'm
finally with my bussing bucket out on the floor
stacking sticky latte glasses,
scraping plates of brie-crossaint goo and
mooshed turtle brownie mess.
I
am moving to the next table when
our faces meet like a movie set
—the door swinging open right onto *there she is*—
the girl
kissing Alec in Freya's photo,
the alienishly tall redhead: *her.*
the one I saw—yes I know for sure—
at the Lake House
two weeks ago in the kitchen as I
bolted from the party angry at Alec
and hating my life.
I saw her standing there—see her standing now—
and thought
how pretty she was,
and strange, with those red eyebrows.

Last week too—before I knew—
I served her cake.
She came in and
ordered decaf. I thought
it was interesting she was alone.
But now she is here—alone—and all I can think is
I am going to faint and then throw up.
Or maybe throw up and faint.
The rush of blood to the head is so strong I can't see
and then I can't move,
which is when she strides past
—almost close enough to touch—
in her smooth-fitting jeans,
her equestrian boots, and a cashmere wrap that's
   going to swallow her.
She is all slow motion:
red hair heaped up on her head, not even
wearing any makeup.
I am going to
collapse. My whole body is
shaking
but somehow I am bolting
—my rag still wet on the table—
to the kitchen and the giant walk-in cooler
where I squat among the bins of pre-cut lemons,
the quarts of organic cream,

wrapping my arms around my shins
—my face pressed in my knees—the cold giving me
a real reason to shudder.
I gulp in
big breaths of dry, cardboard-smelling air.
I want to cry
but I can't.
I am already going to be in trouble
for leaving Margot out there,
for abandoning my post.
I cannot cry.
—I must go back out there I can't stay in here
    another minute—
I cannot cry.
—I will never stop crying—
I can't.

Borrowed Determination

Emerging finally
from the safe, dark caverns of the kitchen
—damp-faced and still shaking—
unsteady
on my feet,
I am unsure
if I can face
the face
that just waltzed in.
What's wrong with you? Margot says
with more disgust than concern—
making Nadia turn,
bringing the crying in me all over again.
My friend is
immediately
two small hands on my shoulders,
face set with strength.
She's here, I whisper. *She came in.*
(Trailing unstoppable images of
her face-his-face-their-hands
behind her, reeking the perfume of
he-picked-me-not-you.)

Nadia's tiny fingers squeeze
into my muscles,
she whispers
—but it is a warrior scream through my spirit—
You will not let her beat you.

Staring Contest

Does she have eyes
in the back of her head? Brown glaring mean ones
under all that red hair?
Is she somehow watching me
—watching her—
without moving a muscle,
without lifting her chin,
not even when
I overheat
a whole carafe of steamed milk that bubbles over
    everywhere and
Margot says *Shit* loud enough to hear?
She must because the rest of her is
unmoving,
uncaring,
and perfectly blank—seeing, I guess
who can outcool who,
who can do it without ever
losing
her cool.
If so I am already losing.
If so she doesn't have to rub it in.

She can't have
just walked in here, she has to
know who I am. (She can't have just walked in.
Why else is she here?)
Maybe she is waiting
for me to say something first, is challenging me
in some secret code I don't know.
By now the back of her head
must be burning
from where my eyes are boring holes into it.
Soon her whole face will be on fire,
and she will look over, melting.
But no—
after two hours on that laptop she gets up, glides out,
doesn't look back or sideways,
leaving me alone at the counter
the image of her burned in my eyes
for a very long time.

Secret Knowledge

After work I want to call Freya
—call someone—
since I can't call Alec. I want to say
She came in today;
I know her. And she doesn't know me.
I want to tell a person
who isn't Nadia, someone
who will have a little more
Ohmygod in their voice, someone just as stunned
and astonished
as I was this afternoon,
someone who'll want to hear
all the mean things inside me,
who will throw in one or two things herself.
Telling Freya though
will mean telling
half the school,
and I want to keep this to myself awhile:
a small stone of poison to roll between my fingers—
unsure how to use it
unsure
how much harm it could do.

Called Out

As the rest of my chemistry class
pulls desks together
for group problems,
Mrs. Baetz stops at my desk and
asks me into
her office
at the back of the room.
I have only been in here once before,
last year
when I assured her I understood
how far ahead I was
and she could help the others
without any guilt.
Now she is guilty-faced again and
leaning forward on her knees.
She wants to know
am I okay?
What I like about Mrs. Baetz is
how she leaves me
to do my thing,
so this intimacy is weird.
I am not sure

where to look.
I tell her I am fine.
On her desk
a stack of yesterday's tests, waiting.
Mine on top
—a sad, red C.
The numb feeling replaces
any shock or shame.
It could be anyone's test there;
what does she want?
Just personal stuff, I finally give her,
and the chair squeaks
as she uncrosses her legs.
I can feel her
deciding about me.
I hope personal stuff now, she finally says,
won't ruin your good future, Becca.
My head jerks up,
staring her full-on.
Now *was* my future
and it is already
very much ruined.

Bootstraps

When the phone rings after dinner I am
dry-eyed and empty on my bed,
staring at the ceiling
trying to pretend it's not Friday.
I am so startled I answer
without looking;
brother's *Heya kid*
is a strange surprise.
You know he's a bastard is the first thing he says,
and it is so embarrassing
(Mom told him)
and so sweet
(he's calling me)
that I laugh.
I start to ask him
why do boys do this?
What is the appeal
of someone shiny and new?
But instead he surprises
when he goes on:
I can also guarantee
he's pretty eaten up.

This gets my
attention,
and he explains how
—invisibly—
Alec's just as smashed-up as I am.
Because love wrecks us too, kiddo—
we just wear it different.
Sometimes
a lot worse,
because it's on the inside.
The thought of
Alec sad
makes me sad
but it also feels better,
and Ian telling me anything
about his hidden secret heart
is enough to make
a lot of other things go away.
We change the subject to roommates and classes
and then he says, *bootstrap time* before he hangs up.
It was our mantra together
when mom and dad got divorced
when we forged signatures,
learned laundry,
put ourselves to bed.
So since he actually called

—and will be here
for his spring break
in another
couple weeks—
I decide,
for my brother,
to grab my bootstraps.
It is time to begin
the hard haul up.

Sighting No. 2

Saturday and this time I am ready.
Although—
what they call her hair
is a cascade.
No one really looks
like a shampoo commercial
except her.
Too bad that front tooth is chipped—her one flaw—I
wonder if she caught it on a button fly
or zip?

Thirteen Ways of Looking at a Redhead
(with apologies to Wallace Stevens)

i.
among twenty needy customers
the only moving thing i saw
was the eye of the redhead.

ii.
i was of three minds,
like a triangle
in which there are two couples.

iii.
the redhead whirled in the afternoon rush—
it was only a small part of her deceptive pantomime.

iv.
a girl and a boy
are one.
a girl and a boy and a redhead
are none.

v.

i do not know which to prefer,
the beauty of sheer rage
or the beauty of quiet repression—
the fake smiling
or the grimace behind her back just after.

vi.

condensation filled the long windows
with cloudy warm haze.
the shadow of the redhead
crossed it, to and fro.
the mood
traced in my shadowed face
an unmistakable hatred.

vii.

oh deceitful men of tucker,
why do you imagine golden redhead birds?
do you not see how the brown-haired sparrow
would still sing so sweetly
at your own feet?

viii.

i know noble friends
and knew a lucid, inescapable love—

but i know too,
that the redhead has become involved
in all i know.

ix.
when the redhead moved out of sight
she was always there at the edge
of one of many circles.

x.
at the sight of the redhead
leaving in green evening light
even the un-wronged
should cry out sharply.

xi.
she rode over decatur
in a glass coach.
once, hatred pierced her,
in that she mistook
the shadow of her next customer
for the redhead.

xii.
the traffic is moving
the redhead must be scheming.

xiii.
it was evening all afternoon.
it should have been snowing
and it was never going to snow.
the redhead sat, unknowing,
in the leather chair.

Camille

different environs

the coffeehouse is crowded today, not like last time when
you had nearly the whole place to yourself and there was that
thrumming cello music going on. but the crowd is a good
thing, because it gives you something to watch: moms with
strollers—ladies grabbing tiny hands filled with crumbs. one
small boy in green corduroy overalls waves a squeezy boat over
his head, squeaking, his mother reaching for it—her friend
trying not to laugh. but it isn't just them here—the minions of
motherhood—there are slumped guys with laptops and spike-
hair and indie t-shirts and i-didn't-shave-today shaved faces.
high school girls in their skinny jeans and high boots are here
too, plus dough-faced women in outfits that want them to still
be thin. everyone is talking, all talking—though the place is
spacious enough so you can't really hear much of anyone—or
else they're tapping at their keyboards like you, but the music is
again good which helps you ignore everything, and the leather
chairs all broad and deep, so even if there's someone sitting
right next to you, you can half hide. if luli were here you'd be
sharing a doughnut. she would agree with you that the tall guy
with the tiny dreads and the buddy holly glasses behind the
counter—his name tag says stan—is completely hot, and she
would maybe notice like you the young girl back there, the one
your age, the one who doesn't seem to know what she's doing,
whose hand was shaking when she handed you your cake.

the hippie boys and their guitars

and their messy hair and their too-big pants and their little squinty eyes behind maybe a pair of spectacles or maybe just shining underneath heavy eyebrows—these boys and their mildew laundry oily hair patchouli smell, their filterless cigarettes and their open knees, hunched backs. they come in and they get their coffee and sneak eyes at the laptop guys, wondering which one of them might be cool enough to buy them a beer. they nod their heads at each other and stuff butts into ashtrays and move their crooked-teeth mouths together in laughing across the land from here to california to texas and new jersey and back. all around the nation you can hear their donkey laughter, their dirty-fingernail strumming, their weak-voiced courtings and murmurs, their converse sneaker shuffling, all of it blending together in one big stinky sad song of brotherhood.

blindsided

you didn't even have your laptop open—you were so far away
from thinking about writing or memories or things you want
to forget that it isn't—well, it is—funny. instead you had your
head in your french book, your cake plate scraped clean and
your coffee cup needing you to get up and buy a refill. you were
an innocent bystander—you were not watching or listening as
the black cadillac of memory came hurtling toward you, racing
for the curb, leaping up to strike you full on and knock you
down, leaving you coughing and collapsed in a haze of exhaust,
its speakers still cooing that stupid, stupid song—that "girl
from ipanema" that takes you back to that one afternoon in his
dusky chicago bedroom every single goddamned time.

laney's new dog

when a new person comes in to look at the dogs they all
know it, all their eyes going toward the door at the same time
their black wet nostrils twitching long before you hear the
heavy metal squeak of the hinges, before the jingle of lily's
keys. you are never sure if you are supposed to disappear or
not, should continue cleaning cages or jump up and make
yourself vanish into the back room where there is a pile of
metal dog bowls for you to wash. but you like to stay, to listen
and to watch crouched down below eye level on the floor,
wiping the same already-clean spot of the empty kennel over
and over, your body taut and waiting like the medium-sized
dogs—the ones who are excited and hopeful but know they
need to hold themselves still to be really seen. they have all
had their pictures taken, are all smiling their best smiles up on
the shelter website and they know to bring them out today as
the lady in the pale gray pants leads a little girl in a corduroy
jumper by the hand. the girl is afraid of the dogs she is afraid
to be here and the mother is exasperated in the first five
minutes. this is not how she pictured it, not how she thought
it was going to go. *come on laney we need to choose one honey.
don't you want a dog at mommy's house too don't you want to help
her pick a new friend?* but the girl has her own dog and she
does not need a new one. *i want dapples,* she cries, *why can't*

I bring him? and you can see the slight curl in mommy's lip, the way she pushes her bangs back from her forehead and says that dapples is *daddy*'s dog and mommy's new house needs her own—you can see just in that motion how it all went down between them, her thinking now that the idea of anything related to daddy crawling up into bed with her would be worse than eating live slugs. you see this in an instant—the dogs see it too—and you want to go over to the girl and put your hand on her shoulder and tell her gently there will be no bringing the family dog into a house now divided, to tell her she is a girl treading bridges now, suspended high over the jagged rocks where there are sharp winds—and that she can take it from you she will want a friendly puppy on either side to greet her. she will want someone who'll be there when she gets across, wagging his tail.

baseball reject

let's go back to the beginning, play it slow and stop at the
essential moment—the moment he finally saw you sitting
there. first, let's start with you actually looking up his school,
squinting at the screen, finding the sports page and hunting
down the baseball schedule, figuring maybe he's just been
too busy and tired with practice, maybe it'd be cool of you to
just show up at his game, casual and easy—you like baseball,
you are interested but not too. then let's zoom in on your
googlemapping skills, how you typed in the address off the
opposing school ("games listed in red boxes are AWAY") into
the search bar and traced the white lines with your finger until
you figured out how not-far it really was. let's focus on how
you printed out that map, how you even smiled, picturing his
face in pleased surprise—how you thought maybe after you
could go grab some french fries, hang out a little more. we'll
skip over the part about you driving, forcing yourself to stop
at buddy's and get a giant coke, making yourself wait while
all seventy-two oz. filled s-l-o-w-l-y so you wouldn't get there
too soon, so that they'd already be playing when you arrived.
we'll skip too over the wretched faces of his teammates (their
devious delight), the snickers and the elbow shoves when you
showed up. instead we'll play over and over again—that
hideous slo-mo conversation: him trotting over after the

second inning, not even smiling, telling you it's not a good idea, he can't concentrate if you stay, then turning his back on you—not even waving—waiting for you to go. fast forward through you walking alone back to your car, slamming your head against the steering wheel, feeling the embarrassed—and embarrassing—pricks of shocked little tears. in fact, let's not even replay that. let's erase it instead.

baseball players are bitches

you never knew they were so much like women. girls, really.
chattery, nasty, gossip-loving, rumor-hounding sixth-grade little
girls. they might as well have pleated minis on out there, for
all their gum-snapping, lip-smacking cattiness. if they'd ever
been around him at the lake house you would've at least been
warned. but they must've been too busy sticking their faces in
each other's faces, their noses in everyone else's business. that he
is their ringleader—that he's the one they look to—doesn't place
him above them, it just makes him their queen.

and what about that?
the cackling shortstop, slapping the catcher on the butt as the
team trotted from the dugout, lifting his smart-ass smile in
your direction and congratulating the catcher on the grand-
slam double-play?

counter girl conversation

she asks you how your day's been and you have to pause, take
a second, because her face has something in it, looking at
your face—like it's a real face wondering how your day *really*
was, and not just an extra-friendly coffee girl chatting up the
customers. she seems honest and hard-working and her skin
is clear and her round hazel eyes are glossy and sharp, and
you know you know her from here, but you're not sure you'd
recognize her if you saw her on the street. her face knows your
face but you do not really know hers. you have never seen
it relaxed above real clothes, for example, only in this white
t-shirt khakis-or-jeans look she has for the coffeehouse. you
might not know her without her apron. she is still watching
you with that intent look. apparently you have been talking for
a couple of minutes without your knowledge, telling her about
the puppies, telling her about reading french, saying nothing
about the hideous baseball game you just left, about the sting
of rejection that is probably still burning on your cheeks. it
strikes you though—something about her—that maybe one
day you could. she takes your money, hands you your coffee,
your cake. and you find yourself sneaking glances at her now
and then. there is something in her face today—looking so
seriously at yours—that you don't know but want to.

Becca

Flirting with Disaster

It's like
dangling a steak in front of a Doberman:
she might lick your face,
she might
bite off your hand.
But what are friends for, if not a little
danger and sympathy?
So I finally tell Freya
about the redhead at the coffeehouse.
Maybe I want compassion
—maybe I just want
to see some blood.

The Plan

Freya says it's simple—
a classic kind of plan:
your friends close,
your enemies closer,
close enough to twist
the horrible knife plunged once in your back
immediately back
into her heart.

Iago's Daughter

The only way
to repay a traitor
—Freya says—
is to betray her.
It is
a good way too to get back at Alec,
a way to
show how tough
—how over him—
I am.
And though I am not sure
two untruths undo each other,
though this
befriend-her-then-bushwhack-her plan is
a plot more plausible
in one of Freya's magazines,
I want someone to hurt
and it might as well
be the girl who hurt me.

The Elephant at the Dinner Table

It's been
a couple weeks since my future
got snapped off like an icicle tip
and tossed in the street.
Mom is a lined forehead across from me,
a knobbed hand
against a pointed chin.
The ghosts of *Will you still do FSU now?* and
If not, where else do you think? drift around us,
forlorn and silenced—unattended and
ignored.
My mouth is a hard line set against her,
but my response hides under the dinner table,
crawls deeper into my lap;
it is small and shivering, and I cannot
look at it—this fearful answer inside me:
I don't know.

If We Practiced

Looking around first period with new
—red-rimmed—eyes I see
how alone I still am.
Jenna—for example—I know only
because of roll call, how her
eyebrows press together briefly
before she half-whispers, *here*.
Like me she is mainly
head-down, back-hunched.
The only two girls in a class of
acne-scarred hopefuls, it is better if we don't
call too much attention to ourselves.
After lecture when we are
loosed outside onto the concrete and
allowed to disappear
through the illicit cords of our iPods
and the callous-building on our strings
she is
always farthest away on the steps
her body tall and long—a praying mantis girl,
whisper-singing to herself
so quiet, only she can hear.

Neko Case sticker on her notebook—
I imagine myself asking her about it,
maybe
ending up at the concert together
maybe taking down notes
—copying chords,
rehearsing after school, getting so good we
ask Mrs. Fram if we can use the recording stuff.
Jenna would show me how to work a slide.
We would play at Eddie's Attic.
I have time to rehearse now.
We could be really good.
If I could only get her
to look at me.

Puppetmaster

Next time I see the redhead
the fury hides
behind my tongue
twisting my mouth somehow
into a grin.
I'm a puppet of my own pretending,
a ventriloquist of deceit.
Cute jacket comes from someone else's voice
—my voice—
my eyebrows in an attempt
at being sincere.
She shrugs one slim shoulder,
and I feel Freya's hands in mine,
wanting to wring her neck.
I never know what to wear in this weather,
the redhead says.
At least in Chicago it's always cold.
The marionette strings strain
as I hold myself back
from asking
if that's how she stays warm:
curling herself

up in the arms of other girls' boys.
At least you've always got coffee comes out instead
—my own brightness blinding
my narrowed wooden eyes.
This tightrope between us,
a taut beginning, at least.
Later,
jerked-on joints propel me
to sneak her cup, wink,
and fill it for free.
When she lifts her face in thank-you
I almost have to use my two fingers
to prop the corners of my mouth
in a mirroring smile,
and not dump the coffee
right there
in her lap.

Balance

She bites her nails when she writes.
Her skin is
unfair,
not to mention the rest of her.
But I have this on her—her childish habit.
It is hard not to ask
what she is so nervous about
—what unholy thing she's done—
that drives her to chew her hangnails,
what dark part of her insides wants
to make herself
—at least a little—
ugly on the outside, too.

Night Shift

Eleven on Thursday and we have
the stereo booming
to some fabulous old rap.
The coffeehouse is finally closed,
and I have forgotten all about the redhead,
just doing our closing chores:
Nadia wiping the wine counter down,
Denver clearing the dishwasher,
me bopping with the mop
across the floor
pretending that I
know this song.
Seeing me
Nadia stops:
comes around the counter
popping her hips.
She screams the lyrics for me,
grabs my mop arm and
we start to swing.
Denver comes jumping
up and down from the kitchen
and we make a circle

one-two-three-and-the-mop

a goofy ring-around-the-rosy all the way down

to the sudsy floor,

both of them shouting dirty lyrics and laughing

until the song is over

until it's time to get back up.

I finish my mopping, head to the bathrooms

with my rubber gloves.

Nadia's cleaning

the cake cooler now.

Denver will go disinfect

the rest of the kitchen

while Nadia counts the money,

and we lock up.

We'll go to our own houses,

back to our own lives.

But on the sidewalk, saying good-bye, our faces are

   beaming

—none of us sure

what happened in there, but

all of us obviously

insanely glad.

Surprise Flare

Just as I slide
in between the cold sheets, nestle
my clean, wet head onto a pile of down,
a quick thought flashes
across the back of my eyelids, an image so bright
and sudden
I almost gasp.
It is me kissing
a mouth that's not Alec's.
Another hand skimming my collarbone,
someone else's legs—Denver's—
wrapping around mine.
It is a comet of a thought:
fast and fleeting,
bright but brief,
and leaving a burning hot trail behind.

TGIF

Sliding into clean jeans,
a fresh turtleneck,
and having the clarity
—without coffee—
for a little mascara,
I look at the mirror and realize
it is Friday again.
Somehow
I not only know
what day it is, but also
I have reached
the end of another week without him,
with the wherewithal
for clean clothes
and a hairbrush.
Two weeks ago I could barely crawl
through the clouds of despair
clawing at my body,
making it hard to breathe—
no sleep
little food
nothing but pain.

Impossible
to stop crying
—impossible
to even take a shower.
But today my eyes are clear and
I care about my socks.
I've been
eating breakfast
for the last two days,
and my stomach growls now,
waiting for me to catch up.
It's a small triumph,
and there's farther to go,
but as I glance in the mirror
one more time
I see myself,
give myself
a tiny smile.

Two Girls at Loose Ends

It's Friday night, Mom says,
home from her hospital shift,
seeing me
on the couch,
glaring at an issue of *Poets & Writers* I'm not enjoying.
What're you doing tonight? she merrily wants to know.
When I shrug
—nothing—
suddenly the world tilts:
we are
calling Fellini's,
in the car to the video store,
come home with
her favorites—*You've Got Mail,*
a feta-onion-spinach pie,
a carton of Milk Duds, and
another movie with Cate Blanchett.
We are
quilt-pillows-pajamas-pizza pile
on the sofa together with our knees touching.
She is

a woman of delight I haven't seen in a while. I am
a relaxing version of myself
I haven't seen either.

Camille

empty

quick, without thinking about it too much, list all the things that are empty: coffee cups in the sink; a pair of dirty jeans on the floor; lockers on the last day of school; baby bottles sucked dry and tossed out of high chairs; playgrounds on rainy days; movie theaters at 8 a.m.; photo frames with broken glass; libraries after a fire; hands with no one to hold them; a dead woman's jewelry box; your mind when the sun is just right and the music is good and you've just sucked the last bite of cake from your fork; a car parked in an alleyway next to a jazz club, where everyone inside is smoky with sweat; taxis with off-duty lights; a long road in the middle of the texas desert; the sky of stars in space; the beach in winter; a stranger's eyes on the bus; both your inbox and your mailbox, of any message you might want to receive, save this—two lines from the catcher, cryptic and confusing, and yet maybe a comfort—*seeing you is too much. what about saturday?*

the coffeecounter girl

—the one who's your age, the one you like seeing here because
you know, like you, she doesn't quite fit in—has an anger in
her throat, but her laugh comes out like a ribbon from her
sometimes—the way she guffaws at the barista and can barely
contain her crush behind her hand whenever that scruffy,
impish college boy with the bandana for hair comes out of
the kitchen, how she asks you every time how your day was,
her smile a kind of bright that makes you want to squint. but
when you are watching her and no one else is, she is placid and
calm as a landscape painting, enjoys the sliding of warm yeasty
things from racks to trays and from trays onto plates or into
bags. her favorite is the heft of a muffin in her hand just before
she squeezes it. she seeks the peaceful yawn of doughnuts,
smiles at the hissful blissful steam of new coffee brewing. there
is a buzz around her: the real baristas aswirl in their espresso
steam, the children fingering the organic chocolates on display,
the post-grads hunched in line, waiting for her itching for their
coffee and their laptops, the cash register drawer with its merry
bell. in all this her eyebrows are smooth and pleased even if
her mouth is always turned down around the thing she still
somehow can't bring herself to say.

yeah, that

what *about* saturday? you decide to sit on it, and don't write
him back.

the amateurs

they took you in so fast you almost forgot for a while you
weren't one of them, but now watching your friends get all
weepy over plans for their last spring break you find yourself
squarely outside them all again. willow's family has a house and
everyone goes; apparently, they've gone every year—have gone
since middle school—and now the volume rises as they start
talking on top of each other, telling tales of old times, doing
the *remember when* thing you'd already like to forget. this is
their last year, this time will be the last time and even though
it is still weeks away, it is apparently time to go shopping for
new swimsuits and this is what's got them all wet. *you come
with us* they plead to you, putting their hands on your knees
and insisting how nice it will make things, your first time being
their last, how you're already one of them, how it wouldn't
be the same if you weren't there. you shake your head and
smile sadly and say something about family, something about
vacation your dad never gets to take. you will not go with
them—will not really go anywhere—but at least you will not
have to watch them flounder and fumble, wet-eyed and weak,
first-timers at detachment. at saying good-bye.

countryshow

mom's moved on to concerts now, and tonight it is neko case at a place called the tabernacle: this old genteel lady of a theater with a chandelier bigger than a mack truck hanging over the center, and balconies draped across its back like strings of ivoried pearls. right away upon walking in your wretched traitor heart knows that boy in chicago would love it, would love the gentlemanly bathrooms and the dowager lounges on every floor. your seats are high enough to see everything but not so high you will miss anything, and when that scrawny gal clomps onstage and takes her guitar in her fist you could swear you feel his hand in yours. you won't linger because it simply can't be said well enough how that lonelysadtrue voice moves straight from her ruby mouth to around your heart and squeezes so hard you feel your knees buckle. but lucky your mom is there by your side, her wide-eyed smile next to you, turning its beams on you, refusing to let you shrink. refusing to leave you alone.

crossroad

after that whole baseball fiasco—and the weirdo nonmessage
message you both know you didn't respond to—you're certain
tonight's lake house deal will not be a date. still, you do know
the catcher will be there. and he knows you will be there. and
you both know that right now you are probably getting ready
to be there, knowing the other one will be there. what is he
practicing to say to you and what are you (really) practicing
to say back? what is "too much"? and how much? and what
kind? you don't like to cross these kinds of uncertain bridges—
drawbridges that may not close once they're opened. this is all
making you too itchy and you need a new route. go a new way,
just get away, or at least don't head his way. and yet—and yet—
he was definitely walking across the little bridge you'd built, he
was definitely coming toward you from the other side, trying
to span something. at least, it really seemed like that. and
maybe still does—maybe he's still trying to. so now you don't
know what you're doing and you definitely don't know what
to wear. the jeans worked before but follow this thought all
the way and be honest: do you really *want* to be kissed again?
really? or ignored and dissed? either one could happen and
anyway that party is always full of so many other people you
could much more easily not be attached to. why even think in
this stupid direction? *(seeing you is too much.)* remember too

there are three unanswered postcards on your dresser—a whole
other bridge made of toothpicks and dried roses that you're
not even sure is standing any more, since you've only stared
into its memory, your heart thumping like mad. so now look
at yourself and make a decision, because otherwise you're just
some dumb girl halfway on two shores with no way to cross
back over to her own island, just some girl standing in front of
the mirror—some lost girl with no map—nothing but a slutty
camisole in her hand.

impossible

it's not that you're hurt, and you're definitely not sad. what
you are is *pissed*. because you are *careful*. you are choosy. you
are a girl with a metal detector in a minefield. you are the one
testing for trip wires. you do not put your foot down unless
you know what's underneath. and so now this is just all too
mortifying to really stand. it's not like you wanted him to
be your *boyfriend*. it's not like *you* went after *him*. you'd just
chatted by the bonfire! and then he was spouting haiku and
revealing his soul and grabbing you on the deck. you are not
the one who started this—you were going to end it first, right
then, tonight. it should be him burning with humiliation
now—who left the party early—not you. it should have been
you who said *i'm sorry i can't*, not him. that he beat you to it is
just maddening. that you didn't see it coming is even worse.
that all you said to him was *i think we need to talk*, and then
got *that* for a response makes the veins stand out on your
forehead. you weren't going to say you loved him, didn't want
to swap promise rings, wear his letter jacket. you weren't the
one who *attacked* him in front of everyone, aren't the one
who should be here alone on a saturday night back at home
remembering his cold face looking at you like he was someone
you didn't know at all—someone else you'd never met, never
had the chance to size up.

even more impossible

and then—and then!—as you're trying to bolt, trying to move as fast as you can out of the room and then out of the house and into your car and out of the neighborhood and maybe even out of the *county* for a little while—still so shocked and pissed and horrified by the catcher's stupid pathetic apology—like he was *dumping* you!—you don't really understand what's happening. because you're going through the dining room, pushing past who-gives-a-crap and no-one-cares when all of a sudden a pale clawed freckled hand is seizing you by the arm and grabbing tight. you think for a minute it might be the catcher trying to explain but no this hand is far too skinny and it's attached to a white scrawny arm and above it is a harpy face you've never paid attention to before, eyes full of hate that know all too well who you are. you can't believe her grip but more you can't believe the utter venom in her face, which makes what she says even more disorienting, and not just because of the cloud of wine cooler breath that comes out of her icy pink frosted lips: *why don't you leave him alone. you've done enough to ruin his life—his and his ex's, thanks to you—so leave him alone why don't you why don't you just leave.* and as quick as that like you are a warty toad or a poisonous slug that might crawl farther up her arm she drops you and teeters away. it's so fast and so furious you're not sure it really happened at all except this morning there are three dark bruises on your forearm from where she was grabbing you, from where her nails dug in.

Becca

Midnight Message

I'm not sure what
time it is or day it is but it is pitch-black,
I'm half-asleep,
and my phone is ringing by my bed.
Seeing Freya's number I have it at my ear, hear:
I told her for you. I told her so.
She's gone now. She'll be gone. He won't touch her.
He left.
And I am half-dead in my pajamas,
but she is drunk
and she is stupid
so I say *Where are you? Do you need a ride?*
And all I get is a tired yawndrawl:
There's a bed here. I'ma bed now.
I hear the sound of pillows,
her dry mouth,
and not much else.
Are you okay Freya? Do you need me there?
And she is a long time answering
—she is probably passing out—
she won't remember what she says next,
but I won't forget:
He left—he left her. She won't be bothering you now.

Freya's Phone Call Sinks In

Going through the *New York Times Book Report*
Sunday morning with Mom—scones and coffee still
    warming our bellies,
shearling slippers still warming our feet—
a sly smile
creeps from nowhere across my face, remembering
—about a week ago—the redhead saying,
Boys are assholes, when a gang of cute ones
with guitars came in.
They cut in front of her,
made a mess with sugar packets,
caused a ruckus laughing,
and left no tip.
I didn't
know what to say to her, didn't know
what to think about
those brown eyes so serious, mad
and a little hurt.

Relying on Reconnection

LeVaughn's laugh.
Hannah's dramatics.
Paloma's patience.
Summer's smile.
Jackson's jokes.
Maddy's hysterics.
Jonah's guitar.
Grace's style.
They are all out there
—in the Monday parking lot—
still enjoying the things
that once made us all friends.
While I am inside
looking out at them
wondering how I
came to this lonely end.
Will they forgive me
if I go out there?
Will they say sorry,
it is too late?
Our senior year

—this is my last chance—
to trust our old bonds
and change my fate.

Renegotiating Terms

Lunchtime and usually
I am headed to the bleachers
or the library
to cram in some homework
that somehow hasn't been done.
But it's amazing
how much easier homework is
when there's no boyfriend anymore
to distract you from doing it,
how much time you have to do
really anything you want.
Like meet Paloma
in the parking lot, to go off campus
for bagels and soup.
The broccoli and cheese is the best,
and do you like bagels with salt? I just
discovered them and I
think I'm going to marry one I love them that much.
She is talking to me
a mile a minute, like she's been storing things for me
for just this lunch—
not just gossip

but personal weird things
like that bagel business
and other silly things she knows I'll get.
I am not saying anything
about Alec (for once)
and maybe I don't have to—or ever will.
Instead we chatter about TV,
she eats French onion. We laugh and giggle,
drive back to school.
On the way to class I want to tell her
Thank you for being here. For saying yes.
But I guess I don't need to
—she's shown me she's always been my friend—
I just need to keeping coming back,
keep honoring
my end of the deal.

Odd

Nineteen
days
since we
hung
up, and
not
one
single
call.
What's
weird about this
is
not
that he hasn't
but
today's
the first
day
I
counted
at
all.

Gratitude

I made brownies.
When she got home,
Mom groaned out loud with pleasure
—*Good God girl, what've you done?*—
but I kept only a couple
for me and for her.
The rest are for Nadia, for me to take to work,
to somehow tell her
thank you
for all that she's done to help me get here.
For telling me the truth
when I didn't want to hear it,
for showing me how to walk
with your head held up
even if your heart is broken, and weeping inside.
For letting me hang out and joke
in the kitchen with Denver,
when it's slow on the floor
and there are vegetables to slice.
For helping me feel the spot where his
smiling maybe-he-likes-me eyes,
his offer to take me out

on a tandem bike,
and his friendly hand touching
my shoulder—my waist
gives me a familiar/strange thrill
in a neglected place.
I want to thank her for being
someone to like and look up to;
for being like the chocolate I used in this recipe—
dark and unapologetic,
strong
and still sweet.

Looking for Her

The redhead's not here.
Freya is
eager for me to jump the gap now. She says
there has been enough time, I should kick it
up a notch.
You should swap digits. Go shopping. You always
like her clothes.
And I can still feel my hand
on that invisible knife,
still want to see blood, still want
—I'm not sure what, but—something cruel.
But seven o'clock, eight
and that's not why I'm looking.
It is way after
her weekly animal shelter shift, something
I know about only
because when I asked once how her day was,
she said *full of puppies* and I asked her more.
I thought then
I might just tell her who I am,
might throw down my cards,
see what kind of ace was in her sleeve.

I don't want
to like her for writing with discipline,
for volunteering
to take care of puppies
and not shopping and gossiping
or whatever else it is rich,
beautiful boyfriend-stealers like her do after school,
but here I am
wiping down the cake cooler,
wondering what kind she would have ordered
if she'd come in tonight?

Kitchen Surprise

After three straight hours
of Saturday *mayIhelpyou* face,
strand of hair plastered
to my clammy forehead and
back/fingers breaking
from the heaviness of the slosh-full bussing bucket,
I slump myself into the kitchen,
dreading the dishwasher's steaming mouth.
I am a sour dishcloth,
a frown from the inside out
until I round the corner and find
Denver in his dirty shorts,
and that interesting tattoo
—his hands working up and down,
his body an arc of concentration.
I am not sure
which is more of a surprise
at the end of this frantic night—
a cute boy in the kitchen
randomly juggling tomatoes,
or his smiling through the arc of them

saying there is
a party at Nadia's after work and
do I want to go?

Runaway Imagination

Bussing tables, barely concentrating,
I fizz with fantasy—
a kind that's been faded for a while.
Those slidesmile eyes,
that knowing wink,
the heat
in his I-think-nineteen-year-old hand when he
presses a palm to my shoulder,
letting me know he's coming through
with another tray of muffins.
If I went back there again now,
glossy-lipped, would Denver press me into the cooler,
strong, taut, slender cycling boy sliding me onto the
    giant steel sink,
squeezing me against the butcher block,
moving those bike-mechanic hands against my—
    where?
A plate clatters to the floor,
doesn't smash but
is enough
to snap me back to here and now.
Clean up the mess, go wash hands,

splash cold water on my face—flushing foolish
in the bathroom mirror.
Retie the apron,
re-enter reality:
me and him so pretend
I can't even make it up.

Nadia's Apartment

When we get there it's crowded
but I don't care
much about the people.
There is the smell of garlic-incense-flowersoap-old sheets
and something dusty I can't define,
but it might be freedom.
There are
stacks of CDs on an old leather trunk,
a laptop plugged into the stereo, and headphones
bigger than my feet.
I can't imagine the furniture ever matching
anywhere else, and on the wall there is
an astonishing painting
of a nude in repose:
huge peachy breasts pushed forward but
eyes blue blanks of disinterest.
On the opposite wall her partner
—bare-chested Jim Morrison—
dances among some small postcards of birds
I think someone drew.
Past this den of cool (books and bookshelves and
    crates of more books)

is the tiny kitchen where open shelves are crammed
with Chinese blue-and-white bowls,
chipped mugs,
heavy white restaurant plates,
and thick Mexican glasses lumpy with bubbles
and blue rims.
Bottles of beer
and ice
fill the whole sink
and my mother would faint
if she saw that dirty stove.
On the windowsill
a Britney Spears doll gets carried off
by a plastic Godzilla,
and two speckled quail's eggs rest in a porcelain bowl,
beside a faded postcard
from somewhere in France.
The refrigerator is covered
with silly magnets and crazy snapshots
and I am dizzy with wanting
to see my face where hers is in each picture,
smiling with arms around
these pierced-nose, spike-haired friends.
Someone hands me
a giant Mason jar—bits of mint float on top.
The taste is thick with sweet, and something sharp.

Later in the bathroom
with its tiny vintage tiles and
cracking pink pedestal sink I
keep myself from peering in her medicine cabinet,
looking through her toiletries,
and instead stand staring in the mirror
even my very reflection
wishing to be Nadia too.

A Real Party

At a real party there are
bottles of red wine and white,
corkscrews and real corks
instead of wine coolers
and twist-off caps.
No one break-dances
in the middle of the kitchen—
no one break-dances
anywhere.
They all bob their heads
and move a little
but are much more interested
in intelligent talk.
At a real party people bring
their own six-packs
to put in a cooler
or in the sink.
They don't charge money
at the front door
to pay for the keg
crammed in the back room.
At a real party no one sneers

if they've never seen you.
They are friendly
and ask your opinion—they shift around chairs
to make more room.
At a real party no one is smoking
those stupid Swisher Sweets
or coughing on cloves,
just pretending to inhale.
Instead they have Zippos
and fancy metal cases;
they tip their heads back,
don't exhale in your face.
At a real party your friend
introduces you to her boyfriend,
so happy she knows you
and glad to show you off.
At a real party you can talk freely;
you don't have to try
to be something you're not.
People listen, and they include you.
You can also make eyes
at the boy who asked you
and maybe he will smile back
instead of pretending not to see.
Finally when it is so late
and you have to get home—

you will climb into bed, smiling,
your mind dancing with the pictures
—so many, so swirling—
of your first
real party.

Camille

crashing

it all makes sense and now you just want to disappear. those bruises on your arm, the sadness in his face, the strangeness of the whole three weeks all equal one big black hole you hate facing and practically can't. back-pat yourself all you want about how careful you are, about how in and out of minefields you can dart, pride yourself on how clean you can keep things, how you never stain your own pristine white blouse, but look in the mirror and realize this is nothing but a big bloody mess. not only have you betrayed that lovely boy in chicago—he'd despise you if he knew what you were doing to forget him— but to make it worse you are now someone else's cheat. by trying not to step in the quicksand you've fallen off a cliff, onto a pile of daggers coated in burning acid. so now you are the biggest fool. and worse, a hateful fool. you knew so much but you knew nothing. now everything crashes around you and for the first time you look at yourself and know that you deserve it. you deserve to feel this smashed.

hooky

facing all those faces you are faking being friends with just can't happen today. lucky for you you truly *were* ill with your own disgust for yourself all day yesterday so are plenty pale and wan when mom comes in to wake you. she's got tennis with liz and then some volunteer meeting so you are left alone to drift around the house and float from pantry to couch—covered in blankets—lame tv, a hundred thousand channels of distraction and none of them loud or obnoxious enough to fully drown it out—to drown out anything—because superimposed over the screen you see a replay of the last three weeks, all tinted now in a vomitous green color, everything grimed and sticky with deceit, that bonfire flickering in your mind like the flames of breakup hell you've thrown him and this poor girl (whoever she is) into, the flames where you belong too. they were obviously going to break up anyway if he was after you like that, but you didn't ask to be a part of it, and wouldn't have if you had the smallest hint. you didn't ask to even *talk* to him, let alone be the means for his escape, and now the idea is so unpleasant you have to climb upstairs into the tub, turn on the water as hot as you can stand to sluice off the slime coating that is forever on you now. you are not sad in the slightest about *him*; he can write himself a hundred hokey haiku a day and still in his core he will be just another jock dickhead. that doesn't matter. he's done and gone and you shed no tears for him. it's not him you can't believe, it's you. you can't believe you did this and you can't believe you *let* this happen. how could you let this happen how could you not see it in him how could you not know how could you be so stupid how could you?

the girl you don't know

you're lying on the couch in your bathrobe flipping through *elle* and picture after picture of girl after girl gets you wondering about his girl—the *other* girl—and what she's like. being who he is on the baseball team you figure she must be hot, but knowing what you know about his poetic side you know she also has to be smart. and sensitive. and interesting. and so maybe she isn't that good-looking at all, at least not in *maxim* terms. maybe she's pretty in a different way, like a waterhouse painting or a modigliani. maybe she's bookish with glasses and blah hair and a bit of an overbite. maybe the rest of the team made fun of him and so that's why he went after you. to prove something to them. to prove something to *her*. or maybe, if he was proving something, she *is* good-looking (you are picturing a tiny small girl—a girl like a fawn—with barbie blond hair and huge sweet blue eyes) and too many other people thought so too. maybe you were a revenge hookup. maybe she'd already done something to him. or he thought she might and so wanted to show her two could play at that game. but a girl like that wouldn't have a *friend* like that, would she? (that skinny freckled girl with the big sloppy mouth and the ihateyou eyes.) or maybe the friend was the issue—he hated her, she hated him—but being mr. sensitive-haiku-boy he didn't know how to tell her and you were the way out. maybe she wasn't poetic at all, and *that* was the problem. she had to be something. there had to be something wrong with her. because otherwise why would he have come after anybody, especially someone as horrible as *you*?

affirmation of what you already knew

slow stroll still in your bathrobe for at least a glimpse of the
sun today. down to the mailbox in bare feet even though it's
gotten cold again. the freeze at least is feeling something,
though mom will be home soon and you should clean things
up, get some real clothes on, try to make everyone feel like
everything's getting better. flip through the junk mail—
insurance offers, dad's travel magazines—and head back to the
house trying not to feel disappointed, trying not—definitely
not—to feel maybe tears crawling up the back of your eyeballs.
what did you expect when you *still* haven't written anything
back, have barely been an online presence since you got here?
what did you expect when you're the girl standing by the
burning bridge with a match in your hand? you didn't want—
don't want—anything or anyone and now that's completely
what you've got. so cut it out because you are *not sad* thinking
maybe he gave up and maybe it's over and maybe you'll never
see him again (because you already knew you wouldn't, didn't
you? you knew that you already did). all you really wanted
when you headed down the drive just now was an easy ego-
stroke, something to make you feel like someone out there in
the universe might think you're okay, even though you know
better. you didn't want him, you just wanted what he can do
for you. you didn't want him. you didn't.

unwanted memories #4, 5, and 6

you can't stop them they just come in a constant stream: that
time you cut your last class and got to the institute early so
you could actually walk around together before his shift started
at the coat check and he took you downstairs and you said
you'd already *seen* the miniatures, and you were joking and he
laughed and led you by the hand down the stairs and around
some corners and it wasn't the miniatures he wanted to show
you at all but this other whole room full of crazy drawings—
there was a dali in there, you remember that—all avant-garde
and funky and he sighed happily and said *this is my favorite*
room and you said *of course it is* and he kissed you right there
without even worrying about the guard. some other time he
kissed you too—was it a week later? four? in millennium park
when it was freezing cold and dark so dark early but he wanted
to meet you after work so you went there and stood under the
bean together and in the reflection of that round gleaming
impossible liquid bead of metal you kissed him, one eye on
your bent reflection, reflecting over and over. another kiss—
where were you going?—on the el; you only remember he had
his messenger bag on the floor between his feet and was so
tall and leaning over you, your boots bumping his bag as you
stretched yourself up to his face to kiss him could not ever stop
kissing him or get enough of kissing.

sorry attempt

it's a stupid set of stationery—some frilly set your mom gave
you back when you were writing letters—but it is the only
thing you have. you have paced the house six times and now
mom and dad are giving you raised eyebrows, you know you
look a little crazy. so back up to your bedroom—is anyone
studying anymore, at this point in the game?—and take out
the first sheet. *dear*—, you write, and then stare at it, stupid,
unable to even write his name. you could just e-mail him you
could call him right now instead of this, but you know he has
abandoned his side of the bridge; you waited too long it is too
late, so at least a letter you can burn when you're finished. you
write that you don't blame him, that you'd've left sooner. did
leave sooner. and then your words begin to pour and the main
thing you're saying is *i'm sorry i'm sorry* over and over sometimes
in capital letters. sorry you didn't meet him that second time
he asked—when you left him to wait by the lions while you
rode out to wrigley instead, knowing he was waiting and being
so afraid, you had to flee. sorry for being too eager to kiss him
and then sorry for not kissing him at the picasso sculpture that
day because of your cold. sorry you don't deserve him. sorry
for the last month. sorry for not writing back—sorry for not
saying immediately *you are so awesome*, and *yes*. sorry for not
having better outfits sorry for skittishness. sorry, sorry, so sorry

for having to leave, and for every stupid substitute someone else since. by the end you are crying in earnest and you know you will never see him—you can barely see the paper—and mom knocks on the door to say good night. she sees your face she sees the crumpled paper and she sits beside you and strokes your hair. why you are collapsing into her shoulder you are not really sure but she is good smells and comfort and she only says one thing: *oh honey i'm sorry.*

what you don't know might kill you

in the morning you are not sure about anything. at school
you look around and realize you're surrounded by strangers.
oh you thought you already knew them, but that was because
you didn't really want to know them. and looking around this
morning at this ever-busy hive of bees, you're still pretty sure
about the latter. but they are your friends for this town, the
people you need in order to make the clock move on its axis
and the sun curve across the sky, and you thought you knew
them. knew enough, at least. but you also thought, if the
catcher were off-limits, they'd clue you in in some way, let you
know. now you know you're an idiot for thinking that—look
how they swap around with each other—maybe people with
partners mean nothing to them, or mean something different
you don't really know anything about. you want to ask ellen
now: *did you know? did you?* but what if she smiles and shrugs
and tells you *of course*, acts like you're stupid, decides she
doesn't want to know you anymore, if you've got a problem
with it? take a good look at her now. see all the things you
don't really know. size up simon-sam-edgar too and ask yourself
what you know about them. maybe they have nightmares.
maybe their band is actually good. maybe they don't make the
grades they claim to. maybe they sometimes feel ashamed. look
at jessica. look at autumn. give a glance to flip. you think you

know them, but you just judge them. and though you may be right, you still don't really know. you felt safe in your quick little assessments but now your methods have proven faulty and you've got to try to start all over. because now it's clear you never know what might turn on you—or when all the things you don't know might not really keep you safe.

undeniable truth

this you do know. this you know better than anything else:
you have $7,376.42 in a shoe box hidden in your room. you
have $7,376.42 saved since ninth grade from every extra trip to
the mall you never went on, movie date you ever canceled and
walked the streets alone instead, every gas tank you needed to
fill every snack bar your friends might want you to treat them
to, every allowance, every rare babysitting job you picked up
from here or there—it could be more but it is $7,376.42 that
you have skimmed and saved and in some ways scavenged even
though you have your own savings account, even though your
parents have been adding to it since you were born, but that is
for real college. this, this is for you and you only: not for their
expectations, not for the path that everyone else is going to
tread after graduation, not for any of the bridges you've built
or burned down. it is for you to fly free and go only exactly
where *you* want, when you want, and in sixty-two days (give
or take) you will. you are 18 already sure, but you need to
finish out this high school sentence and then you know you
will take your squirreled money ($7,376.42 now, but there will
be more by then, there will be more) and you will buy your
one-way plane ticket and your eurail pass and explain to your
parents—you have your plan you will spell it out for them
and there isn't a lot they can do—not really—because you are

their only child it's not like they're going to *disown* you, and you've had a dream and they won't have to pay for it—see you have $7,376.42 that you have saved. this you know. you have $7,376.42 and a plan and a future, at least for a little while that will be your own. count it again this you know in sixty-two days you will be able to get out of here you will be off the never-ending gerbil wheel you've been forced to run for your whole life. count it again it is in your hands it is your future and this you know.

Becca

The Perfect Pair

Right after
Mrs. Fram announces
our next project
will be duets,
the boys are looking
all over the room, already
picking partners, planning pairs. I have
eyes for only one person and
am amazed to see
her pale eyes
—silent Jenna's—gazing
pleadingly
into mine.

Jenna's Secret

What you wouldn't know
looking at her—long lengthy lady
with pale hair
and a paler voice—
is that this girl of slinking silence
—this sylph of a someone no one else knows—
is silly.
Out on the concrete we are in our pairs
everyone discussing
what to play in their duets.
My hands are fumbling, trying
to be as cool as hers,
to not make her sorry
she picked me.
What I don't know
is she's already decided our song, and it is
so wicked perfect
I laugh out loud.
Our legs are stretched out
—our guitars are touching—
and she whispers,
Flight of the Conchords,
don't you think?

Acceptance

A strange envelope
in the midst of
two bills, a *Lush* catalog,
and three bits of junk mail
for mom.
It says *St. Andrews*
on the return address
and is addressed
to only me.
I applied there
in November
when Mom insisted on backups,
refusing the only-FSU-with-Alec plan;
it was chosen
more out of spite (and Mr. Burland's recommendation),
not because I could get in
or thought they'd respond.
Now—official college letterhead—one word:
congratulations.
It is like a party
I've suddenly been invited to:
one I completely forgot
was happening at all.

Avoiding

I imagine telling Mom,
and then can't. I want to
but won't, yet. The letter
goes in my rainboot
at the back of the closet,
(the one still caked and coated
with a little Lake House mud).
I am not sure how I will tell her
—how will I tell her?—
that instead of a giant Florida football school
(she didn't want me to go to anyway),
or nearby UGA (where I've been accepted), or even
Agnes Scott,
I want a tiny, private North Carolina one
—a school she's never heard of,
a school that will be good for me,
but will cost
twice as much?

Collaborative Contentment

The magazine submissions are finally collected.
The deadline is passed and
now it is time
to decide.
Sara's idea
—to divide and conquer—
I have to admit
is brilliant.
Instead of making copies ad nauseam and then
taking the whole monster batch home,
—to half-skim—
we separate stacks,
and spend all afternoon—the eight of us—
quietly reading submissions.
Sometimes there's a murmur.
Sometimes a snort.
Mostly
we are engrossed,
and (I think) pleased.
There is
the sound of single pages turning: one
then another. Charlie

clears his throat, Caitlyn giggles,
then stops.
I read a story about an ax-murdering stalker,
one about two dogs in a fight.
There is a good essay
about a family road trip
and two more
I can't finish
after the second paragraphs.
The story titled *Kalends* I circle in red;
It is the best one
—the brightest one—
and I will insist it gets in.
Two hours later
—we didn't know it'd gone by—
Mr. Burland tells us
next week we'll vote.
Rama looks
like a preschooler just up
from his nap
and Sara has a smile
I've never seen before.
That was awesome, Charlie says,
all breathy,
speaking for all of us,
and we all nod.

For some reason next we
put our hands in a big pile, raise them up, shout
go team.
It is the happiest I've felt
in quite a long time.

Working for the Man

The shipment arrived
at the coffeehouse this morning,
but apparently no one has had time
to unpack all the chocolate.
When I arrive Nadia
is on the floor counting,
Paige is three customers deep,
and Stan has called in sick.
I take the packing slip from Nadia,
and the red pencil, begin
marking off *organic lavender, green tea, 85% cacao.*
My grateful friend jumps up and stretches,
takes off for the patio
to snatch some sunshine,
a few dirty plates,
and a needed smoke.
Emmett (Mr. Siegel) comes in then
—a rare Big Boss appearance—
the king of coffee strolling
his royal grounds.
Where's Margot? he asks, seeing me on the floor.
When I tell him Nadia's managing

he heads out
to see.
She comes in too quickly, jerks the slip
from my hand
Get out there and clean, girlie,
she growls from under dark eyebrows—
master's here and he don't like
field slaves
doing house slave work.

Clearing My Name

Crazy Friday night
full of cake-and-wine orders,
bags of coffee,
herds of high schoolers,
dozens of doughnuts,
and everyone paying cash.
What is it suddenly
with the twenties infusion?
As though the president has dropped them
from a blimp overhead.
It's midnight
and only me left
with angry Margot
outside the door.
My hands are red
my eyes are bleary
my knees are aching
and I'm sticky with sweat.
But still I sit here
on a hard stool in the back room
counting the cash drawer,
again and again.

Sixteen dollars under
—the worst count ever—
and unless I find it
she's writing me up—an official warning—
and on top of that,
charging me twice.

Strange Thought

Waking up so-leisurely-late
on Saturday
with no work
until tomorrow
it occurs to me—a lightning bolt—
Alec has a game somewhere
and I have no idea
whether they're winning.

A Different Kind of Distraction

Since this week has been
the triumph of new ideas, I try
something even more radical
for a Saturday night; I call
Freya
ask her
to sleep over.
No Lake House party, no
skulking in the Majestic, but
two girls,
a bag of Doritos,
and whatever else
we can muster.
She says *yes*
right away and
I am then left
to figure out what we'll do.

At seven she's here
and we start making lasagna.
When Mom finally gets in (at half past eight),
we are ready

though the kitchen is disastrous
and the salad is lean.
We tear chunks of bread,
pass the water pitcher
and for an hour straight
Freya grills my mom.

I forget
hers has disappeared somewhere. She
never talks about it and since
I'm never at her house it is sometimes
hard to remember.
Just her and her little sister,
her dad, making do.
And tonight
seeing her
aglow at the elbow
of my own mother I
understand her in a different way,
see her with a different face.
My friend with her stories, her crazy plots:
she is
working to fill something
that will never be filled.
She clings to everybody's stories
—her glossy magazines—

because to her, and everyone she knows,
her own is
too sad.

We clean up the kitchen.
I take her upstairs.
I offer
to paint her toenails
and I am careful with her,
gentle and delicate.
I take my time,
make sure it's pretty
—just like mine are—
just like Mom does
for me.

Don't Believe Your Eyes

Sunday afternoon coffeehouse rush is over and it's
time to clear the patio of its cups and plates,
clean up for the next round
of happy nowhere-to-go patrons
and loitering bored-faced teens.
The clouds have cleared and
a breeze lifts
the pages of someone's discarded newspaper
half onto the sidewalk.
Chasing, I catch it,
straightening up while down the block I see
a familiar face—
not my love but Nadia's:
the man I met
last week at her house.
The one with the sideburns
—the one with his tattooed arm
looped twice around her
and his face
in her neck all night.
Except now he is
strolling

into the Marta station,
his arm around another her
—a her that isn't her, not Nadia,
but someone different—someone else.
They pause and kiss—more than a peck—
disappear.
The newspaper flutters from my hand,
floats, unwanted,
across the street.

Camille

not just a dream, but a plan

the coffeecounter girl is not here today. thursday is her day
you know that but you can't figure out the weekends, don't
know if it's sunday-friday-saturday, because you have seen
her sometimes on each of those days and sometimes not. but
today she is not here—instead it is the tight-faced girl with the
cornrows, along with one of the wan little wispy girls—and
they will not be glad to see you, will not tell you which cakes
just came in this morning, will not sneak you a refill, and so
you don't even pretend—you just turn on your heel and go
back out the door. only now you are here in decatur—now
you are somewhere you can really walk—so you do: first
down to the end of the block and left, though all that's there
is the library (good to note) before things take on that highly
residential look that you know by now only means pretty lawns
and magnolia trees. so you turn back and then cross the street
and go up into the square, around the gazebo where someone
is practicing tai chi, back over and up along a row of shops
and restaurants you hadn't noticed before, capped off by a
starbucks (ugh), but also containing the cutest little bookstore
you have ever seen. you go in—three people say hello to you
right away—and at first you are not sure this was a good idea
because you are surrounded by children's books and the sight
of *lily's purple plastic purse* right there facing out on the shelf

makes you suddenly feel five again, back when you thought you were invincible. but then a chipper, pretty, short woman wearing over-the-knee socks and boots with her jean skirt (she's not a lot younger than your own mom) is by your side asking if you need help finding anything and you smile and tell her *no thanks* but now you feel you have to stay a little longer, at least look around. so you go deeper in the store and you feel like you are in another city altogether, surrounded by buttery yellow and cupcake-rose blue and books and books and all these cheerful things to look at everywhere. to your surprise things open up to your right and there is a little corner full of books for grown-ups. you move—a shark—directly toward it. you hadn't known this was what you needed to do today but of course because there it is: the green-and-white fodor's italy guide facing you. next to it is london, paris—you grab all three of them and go over to a celery green couch. you take out your moleskine and a pen, begin taking notes.

doing the math

a weird prickly feeling starts along your forearms and works its way up to your throat as you read. in these full-color, photo-filled glossy travel books there are sights and train maps and places to eat and museums and guided tours and suggested scenic trips, but it's the numbers that swim up at you, the admission prices and the double and triple dollar signs by the restaurant names and the hotel fees. the price of the rail pass alone almost makes you cough, because it's quite a bit more than when you first made this plan. you realize you don't know how much it takes to travel—dad's company always handles it, always pays for your move—and the kids on the ultimate frisbee team back in sf never focused on that part as they were telling you about backpacking across europe and having a blast. they were patchouli-smelling kids all living together in the same apartment—six of them in there at once—and they had dreadlocks and tevas and t-shirts with holes. they probably hitchhiked, now that you think of it, slept together in parks. but you'd looked into the plane ticket and knew $1000 was a lot but that you could easily save more. since then you didn't think about it and still haven't till now, haven't taken into consideration the drop of the dollar and the rise in gas—only focused always focused on getting out of here as fast as possible and as unconnected from your parents and their coddling and their money and their need to take care of you so long as you're doing what they want. this was going to be yours—only yours—not anything they could touch, not even anywhere they could *reach* you if you didn't want, but now as you drive back home to get to some wireless and to find out for sure your heart is racing and your brain is spinning and all you can think of is that hideous school in houston and that engineer school—purdue—where you applied just to keep mom quiet, to throw her off your scent. you're accepted to both of course but have put off any answer, pleading about berkeley and making mom and dad wait. you won't go to any of them—what if you can't go to europe what if you—but you *will* go abroad, you have to. you are calculating the money again in your head, wondering where there could be more, where you might get a job, if mom and dad would let you since school's almost over, how many pairs of shoes you could sell. you will also stop eating, stop going out, stop going to the coffeehouse if you have to, stop spending one cent. you will save enough you will somehow get enough it has to be enough you have to get out of here *now now now*—and you are really starting to panic for real as you click on one-way tickets from atlanta-to-paris. you think you might throw up on that two thousand number—you think that you might just pass out and die.

what you don't know might kill you #2

you are walking tight circles around your room and your fist is
in your mouth to keep yourself from screaming. you are biting
on your knuckles you are biting down hard and the box with
all that (insufficient) money is strewn on your bed. your door
is locked and mom's knocked twice but you can't let her see
you until you calm down. but you can't calm down you will
never calm down because it was your future it was your plan
it was a scrap of life that was going to be all your own and not
theirs and now it is shattered. and sure you could work awhile
and head out after that, but would you live with mom and dad
then for that long? you were *counting* on this. this was your
plan, something not even luli was free enough to do. but you
are an idiot because you have jumped out of a plane with a
pack strapped on your back and didn't look to really see if there
was a parachute in it. you hadn't thought of that you hadn't
been checking you just knew—there's that word again—you
were going to go, you knew so much and you were so stupid
and now you have no idea what you're going to do.

snapping

when you finally come down mom is quiet and tense but
trying to be normal—she doesn't like when you ignore her
doesn't like when you shut her out. on your plate is baked
barbecue chicken and some almond green beans, biscuits
mom doesn't bother to make but gets from the flying biscuit
because theirs are the best. and it is a dinner you like and one
you told mom to make but now even the smell makes you
nauseous and you press your eyes closed. when dad asks what
the matter is you say you want to get a job, and the surprise
on his face is equaled in mom's. he says if you need something
to just let him know, but when you say *i need a job; i need
something to do* mom leans closer in and asks if it's to buy drugs
for your friends. this is so ridiculous you can't help your cruel
laugh, saying *don't be stupid.* and then dad says *don't talk to
your mother like that* and then you're somehow yelling at him,
telling him he can't control you much longer and you'll do
what you want. and mom says *what is it we aren't giving you
honey,* they want to know what it is you aren't able to do and
she is genuinely surprised and hurt and stunned and confused.
and you can't stand their sympathetic eyes always on you their
comforting hands holding you down, can't stand that the only
plan you really had of your own without them now either has
to involve them or isn't going to happen. you hate this dining

room this chair their faces and you need to get *out*, so you push away from the table and keep going when dad tells you to sit down, that we haven't finished talking. you have never acted like this and you don't know what you're doing now, but you know you are running up the stairs—you can hear your feet pounding—and slamming the door to your room. you start sobbing so hard you can barely breathe.

emergency call

when she picks up you can barely talk—just crying and
breathing and squeezing out wails, and she says *are you hurt
where are you?* and you can hear how she's scared. so you take a
deep breath and say *i don't know what to do*, and you don't even
wait you just pour it all out on her—the catcher, his girlfriend,
postcards from chicago, your ruined dreams. you know you
are rambling and half don't make sense but you have to cover
everything you have to get it all out—she is your only friend,
the only one you can tell anything to, the girl who has stayed
with you in three different cities now. and as you talk the
crying feels like it's coming from some even deeper place inside
you—not your head or your eyes but somewhere deep down
in your gut: a place so deep there aren't even organs there
anymore just a small black space where you've been shoving
your heart. he's gone they're all gone and now you can't go
anywhere yourself and it's just too much to handle you can't
manage any more. there is a huge wet spot on your comforter
from your tears and the drool as you're lying on your side
curled up around the phone and she tells you to take a deep
breath and then take another and she asks where you are and
is glad when you say *home.* she says it sounds awful but she
knows you'll be okay, and she doesn't try to come up with

answers which you think is nice. she tells you to take a bath she tells you to sleep she says that will help and we'll figure things out. she waits till you're ready she waits till you're calm and when she says she'll call tomorrow you are so exhausted you just nod.

Becca

I Owe Her

She told me
—*should I tell her?*—
I had to leave him
—*would she leave him?*—
when he cheated,
—*is he cheating?*—
that it was broken
—*will she be broken?*—
even before I broke it off.

Now I have seen him
—*did I really see him?*—
with another girl
—*maybe just a friend-girl*—
and I owe her
—*she did the same for me*—
the same kind of respect.

I will tell her
—*what will I tell her?*—
simply what I saw;
—*what did I really see*—

I will be her friend
—*she is such a good friend to me*—
and be there for her
—*she is always there*—
in her time of need.

Say What?

What comes out of Nadia's mouth sounds like
Russian
at first.
Then maybe Chinese
twisting into Swahili
becoming Pig Latin,
flipping finally into something originating in France.
I say to her,
Say what?
And she blinks like she can't believe
I can't understand.

When she says it again
—*Yes I know. That's his wife;*
I'm, you know, the
Other Woman—my face rushes red and my
mouth hangs open:
empty
of all the things I wish
I could find any language
to say.

Wrong and Right

I might be an amateur
—I may not know everything.
but I know sense when I see it,
and this sure ain't it.
You can't tell someone
to leave someone
if he's with someone else
when you are the someone else
someone else
is with.

When I say so,
she twists up her face:
You wouldn't understand it. It's—
complex.
I want to show her
my report card
—my straight A's in Chem II, SAT score 2175,
my honor roll certificates
and my history fair ribbon
(third place).

I may not know much about
the *complex* world of grown-ups
but I know right when I see it
and this sure ain't it.

Cleaning Therapy

The coffeehouse is spotless.
I have been clearing
and wiping
and Windexing
and straightening
for the last hour,
avoiding
the constant line six people deep at the counter,
making
Nadia and Janayah
fend for themselves.
I pretend
I am concentrating.
Pretend
to be simple—a little girl who
doesn't understand
anything
complex.
When I finally round the counter
Janayah's face
—as usual—is a rotten walnut aimed at me,
but Nadia is smiling.

I think for a minute
it's all in my head,
until she raises her eyebrow,
smirks,
You done pouting yet?

Scales from My Eyes

It's as though I've been
slapped.
And my face stings and reels,
and the ceiling swims
closer than it's ever been and I hear
some unknowing middle school girl say to her friend:
She thinks she knows everything she acts like
we really like her—
and I turn away,
though there's nowhere to look, they're all
laughing inside their eyes,
laughing at me,
laughing the whole time.

Fist in My Pillow

Once for Alec.
Twice for the redhead.
Three times for letting
any of that happen.
Again for my lost friends
twice more for my stupidity
three times for thinking Nadia
was my friend,
that Denver and I
might ever go out.
Pow-pow
pow
pow
pow.
A punch for idiots in econ.
A punch for stupid Hollywood gossip.
One for people who hate Shakespeare.
Another—make that two—again
for Alec and the redhead.
I punch till my fist hurts,
until I'm
breathing hard and my

forehead

is clammy.

Mom sticks her tired head in the doorway,

says

That sounds satisfying.

She asks

if I will let her

have a go at it too.

Camille

vacant

in the morning mom and dad are both waiting for you
downstairs. they let you sleep late, saved their tennis and
grocery shopping until you finally came down. their faces
aren't angry but are worried and sad and they want you to tell
them what all this is about. if you need money, they tell you,
there's plenty in your savings for college and they'll help you
with whatever else you need. and europe seems so far away
now so impossible to reach; you feel so stupid for wanting it
and for thinking you could go. it'd be too difficult to explain
your outburst—you don't even know what to say—so you just
apologize and blame school, say you're just ready to be done.
and they nod and they hold your hands and they tell you how
proud they are and that you only have a couple months to go
and meanwhile spring break is coming up and maybe you and
mom could take a trip together. maybe even dad could get a
couple of days off. and you listen and you say they're right and
inside you are only ashes there is no girl in here anymore she
has fled she has moved far away.

inbox surprise #2

check ur email 4 onz luli texts later on, and since you are not
doing anything but watching "what not to wear" reruns you go
ahead and log in. there are stupid videos from ellen, random
websites and lyrics autumn wanted to share, photos from dad's
sister, fwds from grandpa, boobtique promos from BUST. there
is no word from the catcher there is no word from chicago but
at the top one from luli: *atlanta here i come.* attached is a plane
ticket—she's arriving on tuesday—and a paragraph saying
she's changed her break plans. she was supposed to be going
to portland with friends but *i'll have more fun with you, and
i've never been south!* you know when she gets here she'll stage
some intervention, she's doing this because of last night and
probably thinks you're insane, but the ticket's been bought and
she's already coming and the black space deep inside that was
your heart flares again and it is better than if you ever got a
bushel of postcards from chicago (or even just one again—even
just one), because this is real and solid and not uncertain and
ethereal, and you feel so happy and grateful you could cry.

cleaning up

at school you were more a clock-watcher than ever, dying to get
home dying to go shopping with mom and load up groceries
for luli's dinner and all the best snacks, dying to help re-clean
the house even though marisol's already cleaned this week. you
can't sit still you want everything magazine perfect for your
friend who is really truly coming, your friend who is going
to travel the tightrope that is strung between you, who'll land
safely on your side, likely a lime green parasol in one hand
and a deck of tarot cards in the other. you are re-dusting the
spotless bottom level of the big mahogany coffee table in the
living room, windexing the mirrors and extra-polishing the dark
banister and even the stairs. you are hanging all your clothes
up, straightening the magazines in their basket, shining every
surface in your room and arranging all your photo frames and
miniatures, all your little keepsakes that have traveled with you
from town to town—the unpainted porcelain frog you made
in first grade, the silly plastic girl with straight-up pigtails who
screams hideously long when you press her back, the strange
double acorn you found in golden gate park the vial of water
from lake michigan, the tiny teacups with roses painted on
the sides from grandma tess, the small leather album full of
someone else's vintage photos that you bought at that antique
place you and mom went to when you first moved here—all

your things so many things you have packed and unpacked and arranged for yourself, but now luli is coming to look at them, your old things and some new things too, and you are vacuuming for no reason you are dusting your spotless blinds, because luli comes tomorrow and you want everything looking just right.

unexpected

in the morning ellen sees you on your way in and stops in the
middle of her conversation with simon and makes a beeline
for you, walks beside you all the way to your locker, chattering
about who really you don't much care. for a while as you stand
there taking out books and putting in others she just looks at
you and you know she wants you to say something but you
are not sure what if anything you want to say back. finally she
says it for you: *hey, listen, what's up?* and you've been avoiding
her it's true, ducking out to the side lawn instead of the quad
with everyone during lunch, taking alternate routes to class
the last few days just to keep from running into her—into
anyone—needing a break from the bees because you're not sure
you haven't been stung, or won't be soon if that's not the case.
you weren't at the lake house; you're not answering texts. and you
are sure if you looked her in the eye her clear blue ones would
see straight through your brown ones and down into some of
the things you're not ready for her to see. so you shrug and you
tell her you are just feeling stressed about school and college
and what's coming next, and then slip in a little truth about
it being weird to be the new girl in the middle of everyone's
big final senior year, when they've all got their parties and
their traditions and the things they've been looking forward to
together since the first days of ninth grade. and you don't really

know why you are telling her this at all and you try to make it a joke or at least not so serious but she has already heard you and then she does the oddest thing—she gives you a big hug and says how glad she is you moved here, even if it's weird. and you chalk it up maybe to senior sentimentality and you remind yourself how she didn't clue you in on the catcher having a girlfriend but you follow her back to your friends and your shoulders—where she hugged them—will still feel nice.

the provider

you check the flight arrival four times in a row before dad tells
you to quit it and just get in the car. mom is staying at the
house to make sure dinner will be ready when you get back
and that means you and dad drive together listening to u2 and
singing loud and happy. it is his favorite band he went to go
see them twice before he got this job with the company and
if you'd been old enough he would've taken you then. he still
regrets not taking you, he says, though he brought you back a
long sleeved t-shirt with all their faces on it. it was three sizes
too big then and still flops around your frame but it is soft and
it is cozy and it was a present from your dad so still you wear
it sometimes although mostly just to bed. anyway he is happy
and excited too—he and mom always love company—and it
is as though your fight with them never happened and though
you can still feel the outline of ash around your heart, today
luli is coming and everything will be okay. in the middle of
"running to stand still" though dad gets this weird look on his
face and when it is over he turns down the volume and tells
you he hopes you know that if he'd known how hard all this
moving would end up being on you he wouldn't have taken
this job. *why didn't you quit when we were in chicago then why
did we have to leave everything why did i have to leave him?* you
feel it all burning at the back of your throat but you know

the exact answers, and you understand why. because it was a good job and so many people were losing their jobs while dad's company was still doing well, opening new telecom hubs in more towns. when people were losing houses yours was still paid for, when companies were making cutbacks dad's still took care of all of you. so they moved you to atlanta, and what else was he going to do he had to go where they said. you know this but had sort of forgotten it all, are remembering the moves haven't been a picnic for him, either. you realize what that job outburst must've sounded like to him: *you've done all this and still aren't doing enough.* you don't know what to tell him—you don't know how to say that you still want to run away from him, even after all he's done.

at the top of the escalator

waiting in airports always makes you think of the beginning
of *love actually*—the scene that makes you and mom cry every
time. now you are in that scene standing on your tiptoes to see
over the shoulder of the big guy in front of you and his even-
bigger wife. the first gush of people is coming up from the
escalators but there is no luli and you're left looking around at
the little girl chattering at two barbies down on the floor and
a man holding a sign that the woman he's waiting for will be
embarrassed to see. there are soldiers in beige camos walking
past and everyone claps and they wave *thank you* and go on
in their line. then comes another push of travelers up the
escalators—the man with the sign strains his neck, the rose in
his hand looks too—people with red bags black bags backpacks
quilted duffels. some people in the crowd around you go
forward to hug some of these people, others turn around to
check the arrival screen again. you are wondering when she will
get there you are wondering will you look different to her, and
the crowd from the escalators dissipates and goes where they
are going, and you watch the girl with the barbies again. beside
you dad is patient and unruffled and smiles down at the little
girl and then smiles at you and squeezes his arm around your
shoulder, once. the man beside you turns and looks and you
look away and your dad's arm goes back by his side. another

push of people—she texted you fifteen minutes ago when she landed surely she is in this group surely it doesn't take so long—and there are brown heads and black heads that aren't hers and blond heads in ponytails and a girl in a corset and another one in a sweatsuit and then there is her face there— then there she is.

living proof

she comes to school with you and at first you think standing
there in the main office that there is no way they will let her in,
that they will laugh in your face and point her to the door. but
she smiles and introduces herself and explains she's your cousin
visiting and she shows them her id and they print her a name
tag that says *lucille*. you cannot believe it, how lucky you are
and you almost run out of the office to show her your locker to
show her the hallways and the wide clean bathrooms. you show
her your first class where you will be going in a few minutes
you round the corner so you can show her your friends. and
in an instant they are all swarming around her and making her
laugh and telling her what she's missed since you've been here.
she is easy and cool with them but shooting her eyes at you—
she thinks sam is too hyper, thinks edgar too cute for his own
good, thinks autumn is just ridiculous and ellen a good choice
of a friend. you see all this in her face standing there talking to
them, wondering a little if you're mixing milk and vinegar but
she is kind and she is laughing and they are all interested to see
what she will tell them about you. you are trying not to show
her off like a bowling trophy, trying not to stand too close, but
she is your proof to them that you existed before—proof you
were a person before they ever saw your face.

Becca

Brother's Arrival

We shine when he comes home.
Not just
bathroom porcelain, fresh-folded laundry,
glossy wood floors, and
clean, well-stocked fridge, but
our daily-grind faces,
now bright with smiles.
With him here
—even for only a couple of days, before
he meets friends in Florida for the rest of break—
Mom's voice is a bird,
hopping
from room to room,
her feathered hands
refluffing her nest.

Brother in the Backyard

It is weird in a good way
to come home from school
and find Ian there,
one leg slung sprawled up
on the back of the couch.
He is smiling-glad-to-see-me,
tired of watching TV all day,
and doing his own laundry.
He is ready to talk,
even to me.
We make Cherry Cokes the real way,
head to the backyard
and the old iron chairs
underneath the fig tree.
It is like old times but not.
Now I am grown-up too,
with a job, and heartbreak,
and secrets of my own.
I tell him about the redhead,
getting over Alec,
about Nadia,
and feeling like a fool.

I tell him about
my secret college
and worrying
what mom will say.
At one point he pulls
a joint from his pocket
and I act like I'm not surprised,
like it's perfectly fine.
He squints when he inhales,
and I try not to stare,
wondering if he does this always
or just when
deep in thought.
Eventually he looks at me, says,
You're
swimming so hard in this ocean.
Don't you know
if you float,
it will always hold you up?
He explains that Mom may freak,
but my grades are good enough
—better than his—
for a dynamite scholarship:
maybe even
a full ride.
That Nadia may have been cool at first,

but she's just a work friend.
Those people are fun,
but not your whole life.
He says I have no idea
what's coming ahead for me
the doors waiting, wide open,
for me to walk through.
You'll understand when you get there,
but I'm telling you
—and I mean no offense—
that high school seems so important
but . . .
And then he shrugs,
done with it all.
It has been
a lot of talking from him,
a lot more
than usual.
It is annoying he's so arrogant,
so dismissive and sure,
—he doesn't have to live with it, he doesn't
have to be here—
but I say nothing,
just sip my Coke,
the cold cherries falling,
hard and sweet,
against my teeth.

Hypocrites Don't Make Good Friends

All Freya says about Nadia is
What a bitch. Then she wants to know
when I'm going out with the redhead,
when we move in for the kill.
But her plan is not a plan to me anymore, just
some silly Barbie game
played by little girls.
I wait
until guitar,
until I'm sitting next to Jenna, working
on our duet.
I tell her
what Nadia did, testing
our own small new friendship,
seeing if she will accept me
and my messy life.
She covers her mouth with her pale hand,
wide-eyed, not believing,
then she strums a few chords, and out comes a song:
Hyp-o-crites
don't make good friends;
hyp-o-crites
aren't nice.

I match her chords on my own frets, strum along,
until we're screaming with laughter,
screaming together.

How to Assemble a Rockin' Literary Magazine

First, weed out
the stupid stuff: the maudlin, the self-praising,
the kooky and plain weird.
Clear the work surface and present
sixteen stories,
twenty-two poems,
some senior photography,
and three charcoal sketches
from a kid
in ninth grade.
Sprinkle heavily with satisfied smiles, let
one or two editors brag about their favorites.
Now comes the part where
you have to decide
what will be first and
what will come last.
Suggest
that *Kalends*
should be at the end.
(Because it is the longest and
because it ends—like the school year—
in May.)

Leave the rest
to the rest of them. Experiment,
test the ocean.
See if it will hold you
if you simply
float.

Practice Good-bye

Before it is even
time for school,
we have to say good-bye. Ian's leaning
out the window of his car,
all three of us waving
until he is gone.
Mom is trying
not to cry, but I hug her and
she gives in.
We hold on to each other
—already missing him—wondering
what it will be like
when next time
it's me.

New Glasses

Just because someone gets new glasses
—and can finally see—
doesn't mean
the world has changed.
Even though I am seeing them
—different—for the first time,
the clouds were always clouds.
Now though,
instead of white blank blurry fuzz I find
rabbits, shades and shadow, wisps and whorls,
a smiling face.

Afternoon after school and I am
returning to work.
Nadia chirps, *What took you so long?*
And I smile,
a quick hug.
She is still
tiny and muscled, still
brightness and sun.
The world hasn't changed,

though for me it is different.
She hasn't changed;
I can just
finally see.

Smoke on the Horizon

And then from nowhere he appears,
a text it's hard
—but not impossible—
to delete from my phone:
life has lost its glow
without the fire of you. let
me relight these coals.

Camille

coffee klatch

you take her to the coffeehouse. inside it is cool and blue and
yellowlit and you order coffee and doughnuts and ask for
them to be heated up. coffeecounter girl is there and she looks
surprised but says nothing in front of your friend whom she's
clearly aware she's never seen. she hands you the coffee and she
gives you your change and you want to explain about luli but
then why would she care. and luli looks around with happiness
and says she's pictured you here and it isn't quite what she
expected but it's not that far off. and you sip your coffee and
you watch her happy mouth biting into fat cakey cinnamon
doughnut amazement and you feel for the first time you
really *are* somewhere—you're really here—and then she says,
okay. now what the heck's going on? and sitting here with her
you have forgotten the feeling of being burnt to ashes blown
away, and it is hard to remember four days ago when you were
weeping but she flew all the way across the country for you
and abandoned spring break, so you owe her something, you
owe her an explanation. so you start where you think is the
beginning, with seeing the catcher, and you tell her about the
surprise of him, how everything was so whirlwind and you
were following your gut, when she stops you with laughing
and you feel yourself blush. *that guy wasn't your gut,* she says
arching an eyebrow and dropping her voice. and she wears

the face that says she's going to lay it out straight for you, and
you've seen this face before and you know how she gets and
you are confused and a little mad and this wasn't exactly what
you wanted her here for, but it's like a kick in the stomach
the words coming from her now: telling you're a tinman who
pretends he has no heart, who bangs around into other people
wielding an ax.

listening to luli

in the dark you are lying there thinking about everything,
thinking what she said and what you said back. she is breathing
soft beside you in your big iron bed and you want to wake
her to keep talking more. but she has said everything and you
have said everything and the only thing left is for you to wait
and see. luli is the trapeze girl, leaping—flinging herself into
experiences and people and life. so you thought she would have
been crazy about the catcher idea, but tonight it turns out you
were totally wrong. *your heart's in chicago, but you don't even
know it*, like it's so simple, *so you're living like a robot and it's sad
to watch. you've got to stop gun-jumping, preparing for good-bye.
you've got to trust a little if you want your heart back.* lying
here now you can feel your real heart burning underneath the
blankets, can feel the blood racing in your fingertips and down
to your toes, with no answer to her other question about what
would have happened if you'd kept *her* at arm's length, if you'd
been a shark then. and yes it worked once in this instance but
she is a rare diamond—most people forget you most people
aren't her. so you have to be careful or else you'll get crushed.
it's better to make a clean cut instead of a tear. you are flying
away soon, you are going to leave. but now the choking tears
come because you remember your sad savings, how it isn't

enough. you probably aren't flying anywhere, might even have to stay put. and with that thought your heart beats hard inside you wanting to get out, wanting to fly, wanting to escape, to go back where it belongs.

speaking to shasta

of course luli loves the shelter, and of course they love her
there. you have been to little five points you have gone up to
phipps, you have walked around decatur you have swung on
your porch. this is the last place she'll see before leaving you
tomorrow and it is perfect and it is heartbreaking how the dogs
adore her like you do. there is cleaning and some scooping
and donated food to put away, but luli's there helping with
her pointy braids and her unflinching hands. then it's your
favorite—taking them out in the yard—and once they're out
of their cages she snatches up two puppies to cradle near her
neck before lily makes her put them down because they need
to practice with the leash. since there are two of you you get
twelve all at once, and the puppies all press their paws toward
you like elementary school kids raising their hands to be
picked. you choose jasper and leona, and belly with her limp,
three dogs new since last week and the sibling beagles who
arrived all at once. last you pick shasta with his sad longing
eyes, eyes that never smile with his mouth because he's been
here for so long. outside you loop them around the perimeter
twice, insisting on behavior, teaching them how to heel. when
they're done with their drill you unclip all their leashes, let
them run, jump on each other, bark as much as they want. but
old shasta stays by you watching the crazy puppies who are

sniffing under bellies and biting one another's ears, luli happily
tossing stick after stick. you crouch down and ruffle shasta
around the neck the way he likes and he flops on his back so
you can move to his belly. you are not sure when this happened
really, when you picked him as your favorite, but somehow
it has happened and as you half-sit there on the ground your
hand going up and down over his tender stomach, his paws
open and his face watching yours—he knows you will leave
him, everyone does—but looking at him you think you might
be getting it, think you might understand.

last words

you are up super early because luli's flight is at eight thirty and
she has to get going to the airport. last night you packed her
and you talked some more, you told her about not-europe,
you told her other things. and she said this was an opportunity
she said it was a sign that maybe your original plans weren't
the right ones and you needed to consider other avenues of
adventure, but also maybe there are other ways to make it
there if you look—you just never know. and you were already
sad watching her jam her dirty shirts into the zip pocket
of her suitcase, trying to squeeze in all the stuff that she'd
bought. leaving's not a new thing to you—you know all about
good-byes—but this morning in your pajamas you are quiet
at the breakfast table nibbling your bagel because sure yeah
you're sleep-bleary but mainly this is one good-bye you aren't
ready for, one you don't want to say. when she leaves you will
be left with everyone else, mainly yourself, and it is rainbows
and candy corns with her but how do you go back to real-life
sawdust and cardboard with your hands still streaky with sugar,
with glitter still in your eyes? but then it is quarter after six
and it's really time to go and dad takes her bag to the car on
his own way out the door. and you can't believe she came all
this way to you, can't believe she was really here and now she
is leaving and you are going to cry. but she grabs you close to

her and she tells you *be beautifully brave* and then while you're standing there in the driveway with your bare feet, waving until the car disappears, her last words are in your brain all over your body reverberating everywhere and blurring your eyes. it all comes together then how she knows you, how she knows, how she whispered in your ear: *just write him back.*

a small chance

heart still heavy with luli gone and the long day before you—
you are not sure you can face the weekend talk, the routine
plans—so before it even starts you decide to just go up and ask
ellen—forget about the lake house forget about cruising—what
about a simple, old-fashioned spend the night? you are ready to
wince with regret, you are ready for her to think you're in third
grade, so when her face lights up and she says she can bring
some dvds you take that as a good sign and make it a date. now
she is on the floor with her feet in the air against your bed—
you are lying on it looking down at her, watching her point
and unpoint her toes. she has taught you something called
pillow flipping you have watched an episode of *family guy* you
are both half-drunk from eating so much raw brownie batter,
and now she is telling you about some guy named hunter
you've never heard of before—a boy she met at summer camp
a boy she is in love with a boy she has been writing and calling
for two years now but who lives in virginia and whom she
never gets to see. and you are up on your elbow now looking
at her like she's grown a whole new face and you must have a
strange expression on, seeing her, because she stops and says
what? like maybe you think *she's* the one in third grade. it is a
worried face you've seen before—a face you know—so you just
say *that sounds familiar.* and now there is a quiet bridge slowly

arcing between you. it is invisible and unsteady but it is there. you are not sure what you will tell her next and what you will keep to yourself. maybe she will laugh at you, maybe she will listen. maybe she will leave you in the end but then, like luli says, maybe she won't.

Becca

Alternate Plans

I was planning to tell her one day soon
over fancy dinner:
chicken piccata, a hearty salad,
those baguettes
from the Mercantile
she likes so much.
But now Mom is home and there are only
leftovers and applesauce.
The laundry isn't folded
and I've got the stereo on
way too loud.
She leans on the counter, says
So about our spring break . . .
We were planning
to go together
to the mountains or the beach,
where her friend
has a house
she always wants us to use.
It is two weeks away, Mom
doesn't know I am hoping
she'll be excited

to see that St. Andrews school instead.
I imagine her face turning purple,
nostrils spewing smoke.
I stay quiet one more moment,
before it spills out
over my trembling hands
in one long stream
of thisissuchagoodschool.
She shakes her head, drops it down,
lifts it again, smiles.
You want this to happen. We'll make it work.
She pours some wine
to make a toast, asks me
to tell her more.

Robomom

The wires and switches in her are clicking—
I can almost hear the hum
of her engines, all the android autopilot
that has gotten her to this point in life,
all laserbeamed now
on me and college.
She hardly eats, paging
through all the information
I brought down from my room:
housing, financial aid, tuition costs, curriculum.
She has questions I didn't even know I'd need to ask
and if her head
had a slot in the back
it would spool out a long tape of calculations.
By bedtime she has a list of numbers
and people to e-mail
on my behalf in the morning.
It is so totally transforming,
so complete—
it's nice but almost
scary.

Springing Jenna (and Myself) from Prison

The sunshine makes everyone invincible.
This morning in guitar
I got an idea—a crazythought from brother
I could not put down.
I asked Jenna
to meet me outside for lunch,
and now I pull her across the parking lot,
my hand encompassing her birdy wrist.
She is drag-foot protesting, but the pear trees are
    snowing themselves
along the fence
and the breeze is a running horse beside us—no one
is sitting inside cinderblock today.
Paloma with her white-toothed laugh
stands beside Jonah's car.
He is in the passenger seat, strumming
his own guitar.
They see us and now we cannot turn back.
Jenna's long white hair blows
across her face, like a little girl at the beach,
uncertain
about an undertow.

I say, *This is Jenna. This is Paloma and Jonah.*

Jonah says, *Listen to this*—

and begins a song about King Kong.

He sings.

We laugh.

The sunshine pours down all around us.

What I Get for Trading Days with Janayah

Everyone's coffeeing on the patio this afternoon
and for the first time, today,
I fill the ice machine twice.
Madras shorts and twill skirts wait in long lines
for lavender lemonades,
and wineglasses aren't red
but white.
Stan puts reggae
on the stereo,
and there is a flip-flop bounce
—a sundress lilt—
to even Margot's business face.
Then a cloud passes
—I think over the sun—
and the temperature drops
fifteen degrees.
My face is frozen.
My hands are ice.
It is Wednesday
and there is Alec
walking in the door.

I Remember You As You Were
(with apologies to Pablo Neruda)

I remember you as you were in the last month.
You were the jaunty baseball cap
and the deceitful heart.
In your eyes the flames of betrayal blazed on.
And the cold rain fell in the cavern of your soul.

Clasping my own arms like a withering plant
the new leaves have softened your voice,
that is anxious and pleading.
Bonfire of surprise in which my anger is burning.
Bitter red thornbush twisted over my soul.

I feel your eyes traveling,
and the summer is not far off:
baseball cap, voice of a river, heart
like an abandoned house
inside which my deep longings once lived
and my kisses fell, happy as embers.

Sky from a schoolyard. Diamond across the field.
Your memories are made of shadows, of smoke, of

a vanished lake!
Beyond your eyes, farther on, the tears may be blazing.
But cold winter rain revolves in my soul.

An Exact Fit

I
thought it was gone
—the need to touch him—
but here he is,
standing on the patio,
during a break I could get written up for taking,
and all I can think,
seeing the muscle twitch
in his bronze arm
is: *my hand*
belongs
there.

Phantom Pain

I took my heart,
cut it out,
and put it
in a box.
It was nailed shut—slammed—
crossed twice with barbed wire.
I bled for days.
I bled all night.
There was no more bleeding that I could do.
It must only be
scar tissue, pulsing now, hearing him say
I can't picture
a future
that doesn't have you in it.
I was filling out housing forms
and my hand wouldn't budge.
There are no more nerve endings in there
—they've all burned to a crisp—
it must only be some phantom heart inside me
twisting now in pain.

Insult to Injury

The nothing I've said
is a chasm between us
—and he will drop, he will
plummet—if I don't say something now.
Suddenly I am
snatched back:
Margot in the doorway, hissing *What are you doing
  out here?*
no time to twist
any words
into a life-saving rope.
I watch his hopes fall,
crash on concrete,
as I'm jerked from the edge, grabbing his body
in one brief—and too silent—
uncertain embrace.

completely unexpected

it is wednesday and it is not your regular night but after group
work in the library for your upcoming american revolutions
project deadline—you are in charge of compiling the notes,
which is better than having to design the poster—you are not
ready to go home just yet, especially since you got to drive.
it was a beautiful afternoon and is a pretty evening so you
cruise a bit down highland and then take some curvy turns
through residential streets—going slow, leaning forward over
the steering wheel, staring at the humongous antebellum
houses with the giant porches and stained glass—until you find
yourself on the back road to decatur, taking enough wrong
turns (and right ones) to find a street you know. it is still
darkening early, but not as early as before, and the sky is
the kind of lavender that reminds you of expensive earrings.
the dark shapes of birds fly across it back and forth between the
tops of sidewalk trees. you sit there a moment watching them,
in your space outside the coffeehouse—as though someone
saved it for you—and in your mind you plan the first words
of a real postcard—one this time you will really send. you are
reaching across to the backseat, you are grabbing your laptop
bag and opening the door with your foot, and at the same time
you see them: a couple in the closed-in patio, the fading sun
outside and the amber lamps within lighting them up like a

diorama play. these things happen—you are not sure of the order, because they come at you all at once: she reaches for his arm; it is the catcher; you slam your car door; a boss-woman beckons; the couple embraces, then he turns away. and it is as though you have crossed into some alternate world, stepping onto the sidewalk. what is he doing here? this isn't right. what is also all wrong is his face—his twisted, sad-gut face as the coffeecounter girl watches him, her own face a broken apology. you don't know what you are seeing and at the same time you understand what you are seeing in the only way it can be understood. it is as though you are in two bodies—one on the shores of disbelief, the other plunging your head under the waves of full understanding—so when he is suddenly too-fast already there on the second open patio where the smokers don't even lift their heads as he's barging past, your own body doesn't move fast enough out of his line of vision, only causes enough of a flicker to make him raise his eyes. and they are eyes you have seen before, empty sad eyes you know, and they turn on you and they know you and they are horrified. he halts, unbelieving, as though you are some ghost summoned from christmas future, and before barreling off again you hear him without really seeing his lips move: *i wish i never met you.* and then he is gone up the street and you are somehow back in your car, the key in the ignition as you stare out the windshield, your heart in your throat.

paralysis

you are still just sitting in the car ten minutes later, staring.
your body is heavy and you can't seem to make yourself lift your
hands to the steering wheel—they are just there, on the key, in
the ignition, where you started. you are not seeing the car in
front of you, really, only the just-now vision of the catcher and
the coffeecounter girl standing together on that glassed-in patio,
both of them sad. you keep wanting to go in there, to get a look
at her, to somehow let her know that now you *know* who she
is, but at the same time you are afraid to ever look her in the
face again. you try to replay every exchange you've had with her
in the last few weeks, but she is just the coffeecounter girl. it's
not like you've talked that much. and when you have she's just
been—nice. sweet. generous. taken interest in you, even. she
must not—she can't—know who you really are, or she'd've leapt
across the counter long ago and slapped you across the face,
ripped your eyeballs out, hurled a pot of hot coffee, driven you
out of town. *what was he doing here anyway—asking for her back?*
and why wouldn't she take him, if she didn't know? none of it adds
up to anything easily understandable, so you're stuck, waiting
here in the car, until something becomes clear. but it never does.
it just gets dark around you. and soon your phone rings and it's
mom wondering are you on your way, and you have to turn the
ignition then. you have to pull out, head back home.

what you don't know might kill you #3

you don't know if the catcher told her. you don't know if she knows who you are. you don't know—not really—if ellen even knew the catcher was taken, and if she did you don't know why she didn't tell you about it. you don't know why on earth he would have gone after you when he had a girl like her or what—at all—their relationship was like. you don't even know really about any of the relationships *you've* had. you don't know what will happen if you try to find out. you don't know what you're going to do after you graduate. you don't even know what you're doing for spring break. you don't know if your friends really want you to go with them to the beach, or if they're just saying that to be nice. you don't know anymore what you really think of any of them—coffeecounter girl included—so you don't know how to proceed, don't know how to act. what you do know is that you're tired of pretending you know everything when you don't know *any*thing. you know maybe now you're ready to learn something new.

There Is Not Enough Weeping

There is not enough weeping
I can do
to fill the channel between us
and swim across.

There is not enough weeping
alone in the night
to bring down the moon
and place it in your hand.

There is not enough weeping
I can do
to fill the channel between us
and swim across.

There is not enough weeping
to drown out the sun,
prevent another day from shining
on your lonely face.

There is not enough weeping
I can do
to fill the channel between us
and swim across.

Reanimation

My phone for days has been
a dead thing—
a child's dollhouse
empty of dolls.
Now tonight, nearly midnight,
it leaps to life—a zombie corpse I'm afraid to touch,
reanimated by his remorse.
Not seventeen syllables this time,
but simply the heaviest one:
please.

Effigy

I sent a straw doll to school today
instead of me.
She can
sit with Jenna and strum with grass fingers,
croak out her dry laugh.
Even her scarecrow brain will be better
at answering my tests,
though her handwriting is scratchy,
and her stubby fingers
can barely hold a pen.
When Freya's crow voice caws in her face
wanting to know
what's wrong with her,
—what's happened—
the red string smile
I pressed between her cheeks
will be all she has to give.
She has just enough brains
to call work at the last minute,
fake a migraine, mumble sorry,
though not quite enough sense
to translate Margot's curses

spat just out of hearing.
At the day's end I can simply
hang her out back,
poke her with a stick
—watch her twirl awhile.
After an hour
I will set her on fire,
this grass girl becoming nothing
but disappearing smoke.

Absentminded

Everyone's leaning over a laptop,
staring intently at the screen,
learning about layout,
uploading all our stories,
and dropping them into place
for the writer's forum magazine.
There's a visiting guest
teaching us the ropes,
showing us about margins,
choosing our fonts.
He is tall and blond and his name is Lain
and Sara's so intwatulated
she can barely sit still.
This is what we've been working for,
what I
couldn't wait to get to,
but now they are all
just goldfish in a bowl to me—
a baseball game
on TV
with the sound down
halfway through the sixth inning,

and I don't know who's at bat.
There is
only one thing I see, everywhere—
please.

A Paralyzed Girl Doesn't Flinch
When She's Kicked

For days the numbness has entombed me
—a mannequin marching
in a life that was once mine—
uncertain, undecided
and decidedly unkempt.
There is still
a swath of cotton around my mouth,
around my face,
and three inches of thickness
between me and the air.
So it doesn't hurt me
—it doesn't pierce—
when I arrive the next time at work,
and am called to the back—before clocking in.
Emmett—Mr. Siegel—is here at his desk,
and Margot is unable
to look me in the eye.
I am told I am
let go.
It's not working out—
I'm not taking this seriously, and there're

too many mistakes.
They have covered my shift.
I am free to go now.
Here is a check
for the days I'm still owed.
He says thank you again,
and that's all there is.
My spine has been severed
so I can't feel my legs
as I walk out the door,
and I can't even turn
to look back and wave.
There's nothing I hear,
nothing I see,
not even Nadia
with her sorry good-bye.

Aftershock

For
six
whole
minutes
I
can't
breathe.
Head
pressed
to
the
steering
wheel—
crying
so
hard,
my
stomach
comes
up.

Epiphany

The fear is a force
moving me home,
driving me
where I don't want to go.
I will have to tell Mom
what happened today,
and she will want to know *why*
and I'll have to explain.
Explain how he showed up,
how I've been making mistakes,
how it's been hard to focus
with everything going on.
I'm two paychecks away
from paying back the car,
the rest would be college—what I was going to save.
I practice the answers:
They just worked me too hard.
What did they expect—
I'm only in high school.
And even in my ears—still stuffed with cotton—
my voice is too tinny,
the words ringing false.

There is
only one answer:
Alec got in my way.
And it hits me, too true,
so I say it out loud,
knowing I can't
let it happen
again.

Camille

hope for shasta

you are out in the yard watching the dogs—two of the beagles
were adopted yesterday apparently, and their sister lopes
around, uncertain, trying to provoke the dalmatian mix and
the boxer called optimus, but both of them are more interested
in the new strange man who stands quietly at the edge of the
yard, the one you've seen before a few times, the one the dogs
think has treats in his pocket. one of your hands is on shasta's
belly and the other traces circles in the dirt, still fixating on all
the stuff you don't know. the man interests you too though. he
likes to come and pet the dogs, to just look—but you are trying
to set an example for them, trying to be cool, trying to make
him do the work. he walks his way slowly along the cinder
block wall, one foot over the other, sidling in his khakis and his
blue diamond tie. the dogs run up to him and sniff his knees.
he reaches down to each one, pats them on the head. but soon
it is obvious he's working his way over to you, and eventually
even shasta's watching when he finally comes forward, stretches
out his hand. *i'm john,* he says, and you tell him your name,
the dog's. *hello, shasta,* he says in earnest, holding his hand out
only a little, letting shasta's hesitant nose sniff toward him. *i'm
not allowed to come home with another dog,* john says eventually,
his eyes looking out at the puppies but his hand still held out
in shasta's direction. shasta, who is leaning over now, licking

the man's fingers. your hand goes back and forth, along shasta's furry back, and his tail thumps once, twice. you don't know what to say and are more interested in seeing what shasta does, watching how he stretches—invisibly—even closer to this new man. his heart is thumping in its rib cage under your hand that rests in his white-freckled-fur, and you want to whisper *he's not that great*, and also *go for it—don't be afraid*. watching him—watching them together—there is a tension inside you that you want to suspend, a sudden understanding you want to take home and bottle, to hold on to and keep for later when you really need it. here, sitting in the dusk, stroking shasta with this stranger, it is suddenly very clear to you the necessity for caution and the deep need to let it go.

hope for you

mom has the letter from berkeley sitting right in the middle
of the dining room table when you get home from the shelter.
it was too weird to go to the coffeehouse tonight—you still
don't know what to do if you see coffeecounter girl again.
i waited until you got home, mom says, though she can barely
wait anymore for you to put down your bag. she doesn't know
this is the only real application you've sent—that you will not
go anywhere if you can't go here—and you wish she weren't
standing here, that you could open it on your own. you didn't
think you wanted to go, but now with the letter here and
knowing their international programs and your squandered
funds and your revised future plans, you are terrified you won't
be accepted. you sit down at the table, slide the envelope to
the edge. if you want to know things better, here is your first
chance. as soon as you open it you will know something, at
least, and that will be a start. you drag the letter opener mom
set out on the table slowly across the top. you pull out the
two-page letter. *congratulations* is all you see.

consolation prize

you spent the last two days working on the invitations: real
ones, with hand-stamped filigrees and mom's best handwriting.
you even dug up your old calligraphy kit and its antique wax
seal, held the match to the wax and then pressed down, hard.
now it is before school and you are handing them to everyone,
even edgar, and they all raise their eyebrows but are cooing
with delight. they won't take off for spring break until saturday,
and before they go you've decided to party. mom's already
planned the hors d'oeuvres and punch and dad's stringing
lights all across the back porch. it will be a real party, a gatsby
party, the kind of party you've never gotten to have in other
cities, moving around and barely accumulating enough friends
to take out for pizza. but now you have a gang of them and
it is your senior year and you are all going away soon, so you
will have this party you've always wanted and who knows how
it will turn out but at least you'll have this. you tell them to
bring music you tell them to dress up, and they are bubbling
and giggling and you feel light as a bird. there are things you're
afraid of, things you can't control but there are also things you
are glad for and what's wrong with that?

purging and leaping, leaping and purging

there's a postcard you want to write but there's something else
you need to write first. coffeecounter girl is not here to hand
you your cake but it's not her day and you need to concentrate,
anyway. you're not sure if you'll send it but it needs to be said:
dear alec, you start, *we were both fools.* you want to apologize,
you want to slap his face, you want to insult him, you want to
say thanks. you type all of this and you type some more, things
you didn't know you were thinking until your hands started
to move. *i was hiding my heart and you were hiding yours too
and we played hide and seek together, and both of us lost.* you say
more than you mean to, you don't say enough. you tell him
about chicago, you tell him about sharks. you imagine him
thinking you're crazy, imagine him understanding, imagine
him ashamed, imagine him glad. you wonder what he'll say
back or if he'll even open it at all, seeing it's from you, and you
type with a fever, you type without fear. you say he's a bastard,
you say you understand. you say that you hope he finds peace
in his life, that he dies alone. you are angry and righteous
and embarrassed and sad, and for the first time in a long time
you're okay with it all. writing, you are a girl on a trapeze,
swinging high in the air. you know there is no one on the other
side to catch you. but your costume is spangly and all eyes are
on you and at some point you'll leap—at some point you'll

flip. and there may be no net—though it may also be intact, you can't see—but at this point the jumping is everything—it's all that you've got. and as you write you understand this, you understand you won't hit send, but for now you are swinging, swinging, swinging wildly in the air. your eyes are open, your arms are outstretched.

wanted memory #1

you'd been dropping by the institute after school and on
weekends—mom had gotten a membership—saying hi when
he was working and hanging out together sometimes after they
closed at five, going to the artist's café for coffee and pie, just
walking around the city—up and down meandering, to the
river, to state street or back to the loop, you didn't care, just
walking and talking—you'd been doing this for a couple of
weeks now. and with him you were never restless but simply
wanting more and more, feeling more at home with him each
time. you could never stop watching that mouth when he
talked, but at some point it got so you almost didn't *want* him
to kiss you, because this felt different and you wanted it to
stay different, wanted him to be *here* and *now* instead of an
escape to somewhere else. he was so tall—taller than you—
and when you walked together sometimes you would hook
your arm around his, and he would always press it closer to
his side with his bony elbow and it was nice. he would talk
about philosophy he would talk about history he would ask
you questions about where you'd lived and where you wanted
to go. you would talk about art you would tell him about
your parents and interchangeable friends, you would go to
the palmer house together and simply look at the beautiful
ceiling. and then one day you were walking—it was dark out

and you were both in your long coats, scarves up to here and he had leather gloves—and you both saw it at the same time: the first flakes of snow floating down against the black glass, and he stopped then and turned to look at you and the snow was floating down behind him, just in little bits and he took you in his gloved hands like maybe you were something carved in expensive wood, and his face came down and your whole neck got warm tilting up to him and you said *what are you doing?* and he was so close to your lips, close enough for you to feel as well as hear him say *something i should have done a long time ago.* and then you were kissing right there on the sidewalk and the first snow was falling down, melting before it even reached you.

a new purpose

$7,376.42. $7,376.42 in a box you have saved, saved and squandered and squirreled and squashed. $7,376.42—each bill every nickel passing and passing through your hands, comforting you, consoling you, helping you fall asleep at night. and you thought it was useless, it meant nothing—not what it meant before anyway, not what you wanted it for. but now you understand it adds up to something different, can mean something else. and it is hard to let go, to imagine alternatives, but you are bold with unknowing, you are ready to explore. so you find yourself online, you are checking out tickets. the price is nothing to you—you have so much saved. you will explain to your parents, they will think it is cool, spring break in chicago. you click *purchase now.*

Becca

I Know I Have Been Ignorant
(with apologies to Dorothy Parker)

I know I have been ignorant at your side;
But what's past is past, and all's to be.
And worthless the day, to linger any more dolefully—
Beautifully it lived, and hideously faded.
I will not write any more of hearts betrayed.
And you, being hurt, may have your tears for me,
But I will not offer you fidelity
You'd be, I think now, a little unworthy.

Yet this is the need of a girl, this is her curse:
To continue to feel, and give, and give,
Because the throb of giving is still sweet in me.
To you, who constant gave me vows and verse,
My last gift will be my absence, so you too can live;
And after that, my dear, we'll both be free.

An End, a Beginning

It wasn't
as bad as I thought.
He called me again,
I finally answered,
told him,
—once and for all—
I'm sorry; I can't.
Now Mom sits,
filling out St. Andrews papers;
spring break is next week,
and we are going up to see.
I have my pen too—
a new job application:
there's more that is needed,
more money to save.
We are peaceful together,
and pleasantly tired.
The future curls up
on our back porch,
presses its back to the door, waits
until morning.

One Is Silver, the Other Gold

Jenna is nervous
in the parking lot before school,
but Jonah tells her
we will bring down the house.
We have practiced for days
and now it is time,
but she is not sure we can say
high-class prostitute in class.
But that's the best part! Jonah cries with a gasp,
and I remember his mom
bringing cupcakes in sixth grade.
These are my old friends,
this is my new,
they are mixing together
like vinegar and oil: separate, but still savory
—essential with zest.
The bell rings and Jenna's eyes
are flung at me, wide,
I hook my arm in hers sing,
Ooo you're a leg-end, Dave.
and she busts out laughing like she always does.
Paloma says not to worry,

as she follows us to the building,
she has seen us together
and knows
we'll be great.

Alternative Heat

Two days and Alec hasn't written,
won't write
—will never write me again.
And there is still a place inside me,
an empty place where once a fire burned,
and lava flowed.
There may always be a trail of ash there.
But that fire burned only
in a darkened cave
where two people
sat alone together.
Out here
in the sunshine
I have other ways to keep myself warm.

Nostalgia

Driving by the coffeehouse
—and I could go in.
I have meant to call Nadia
but it still seems too weird.
I miss Denver and his juggling,
but my little crush was dumb, and he was never
more than friendly.
I wonder about the redhead,
if she's forking up cake,
if she misses me, knows
I won't ever be back.
I wonder if I saw her
if I'd say anything,
or if I'd let her stride by
in her knee-high boots.
I picture her biting
her stubby fingernails.
I hated her;
I loathed her;
but I don't anymore.
I'm not sorry I won't see her,

not sorry she's gone,
just sorry
we didn't meet
in a different way.

Self-Portrait
(with apologies to Robert Creeley)

She wants to be
a bold woman,
an energetic woman
as bright, as brave
as the eccentrics around her.

She doesn't want compromise,
nor to be excessively nice (nor cruel)
to anyone. Just herself,
and final in her beautiful,
her total, embracing of it all.

She tried the angry,
the hateful, the "Oh, let's
stick knives in each other"
and it was awful,
bumbled, wholly inconsequential.

Now she'll stand on
her own strengthening legs.

Her arms, her skin
glow daily. And
she hates, but loves equally.

Camille

the final leap

dear neil—i'm sorry i haven't written before now. i'm sorry for a lot of things, but especially for the way i left you. next week is spring break and i'm coming to chicago. i hope that you'll see me.
i hope you'll say yes.

Acknowledgments

Everyone always thanks their editors in these things, but in my case it is particularly necessary. Anica, thank you for knowing me so well and for cheering and coaching and guiding and suggesting and advocating and in general making me a better person and writer. Next I must thank Andrew and Jenny at Java Monkey, for their excellent decaf and croissants, but mainly for their friendliness and all their helpful insider information. To the poetry coaches in my life—the people who inspired and educated and formed me—this book absolutely could not exist without you: Mrs. Shepard, Mrs. Merickel, Ron Bayes, Ralph Berry, plus Matt (Holden), Dan, Carissa, Brad, Jose, and above all Mr. Davis. *All* the completely amazing people at Simon & Schuster (Bethany, Jen, Bess, Emilia, Mara, Annette, Russell, Tom, Jim, Victor, Christina, Mary, Venessa, Lucille, Nicole, Paul, Carey, Brenna, and Lauren) get a big thank-you kiss on the cheek for the hard work and incredible support. Cara Petrus earns an extra-juicy kiss for the amazing cover and for always presenting my books in such a tasty way. I think I've said once before that I cannot thank my family enough for simply helping to make me me, and the same thing goes here. Nat and Casey, thanks again for the high school low-down. Amy, thank you as always for all your serious counsel, but special thanks for just being there this whole time. Thank you too to everyone at (or in) Little Shop of Stories for being totally awesome. Finally—best, favorite, and deepest thanks to Scott, for bringing the poet alive in me again.

Promise. Betrayal.
Confession. Revenge.

From # Pure

by Terra Elan McVoy

When we get to the Midtown YMCA the music's already slamming, and it's crowded. Twenty yards inside the main doors are throngs of people we both know and don't: kids from youth groups across the metro-Atlanta area, including a lot from Decatur, where we live, plus some who were bussed in from way outside the perimeter, just for this. You can feel everyone's glee to be here, which is what makes JGCC dances way better than ones at school, where everyone's too cool to do anything. The DJ is onstage with his mixing board: some prematurely balding college kid with perfectly broken-in Cons and rainbow suspenders; a guy who likely thinks DJ-ing for a bunch of Christian kids is some kind of ironic alterna-cool, though the joke's on him 'cause everybody's digging his groove so much, he's genuinely getting into it.

Right away, we see Wedge, one of the youth ministers at Morgan's church, standing close to the stage, nodding his head to the beat. There's this ten-yard radius of emptiness surrounding him, like everyone knows about his "Save Britney" website.

Regardless, Morgan bounces over to him, chattering like mad. The music's too loud to tell what she actually says, so Priah and I don't even try to pretend to follow the conversation. We scan the crowd instead: a mass of shirts and faces, people dancing, an arm going up—a head flung back. Out there on the back edge is Cameron, the Methodist poster child for gayness, surrounded by his savior angels: girls from his church and our school who are determined to love Cameron despite his refusal to See the Light (i.e., Convert to the Straight Side). More faces, more folks I don't know—I'm looking for Naeomi's face somewhere out there—and then, *omigah*, there he is.

"Come on," Priah says, just as the DJ starts a remix of some old Madonna, "I love this song." Pree's knack for timely diversions is so keen it's almost spooky, but I don't dwell on it as she pulls me into the crowd and we start to dance. I concentrate on the music, on Priah's big smile, instead of wondering whether Jake saw me, if he saw me see him, if he didn't want to see me, blah blah blah. Instead, I'm just dancing. Or trying to. This really *is* a good song, even if it is kind of old, and Priah's fun to dance with, because she's so good, though not the kind of good that makes you feel bad dancing next to her. I smile back, only occasionally looking over her head, telling myself I'm looking for Cara, and am not, in fact, trying to spot Jake again.

Morgan butts into us then, yammering excitedly, but we just swing our hips and jerk our knees and fling our arms, too happy to listen. She gets it and moves with us too, and soon we are all sweaty and grooving. Some girl from the Unitarian church near my house—the first one my parents took me to in their Tour of Houses of Worship back when I was seven and they thought I should at least be exposed to *some* religion, the one I think they'd attend if they still cared about church—bangs into us and we all smile and wave and do a little dip-you-dip together as a foursome, and the DJ takes us to another hip-hop level, and the whole gym seems to be smiling and . . . just . . . *dancing.*

About twenty minutes later Naeomi has arrived. We open our circle to include some kids from we-don't-know-where, who have this kind of tribal-edge vibe to them (shaved parts of heads, black cargo shorts, chains, "native" tatts on their forearms), and who occasionally bust into this awesome break dancing thing with each other. This DJ has a penchant for the old school, but it's okay because the music is good and my friends are here and everyone is into it. Even Naeomi seems in a good mood. When I scream to her "Where's Cara?" in the middle of the next song, she simply shrugs and smiles and lets this tall Rasta dude grab her hands and pull her into a cute swing-shuffle. I figure if Cara's best friend can take it, I'd better chin up over her absence too.

After another good forty-five minutes, it gets hot—really hot—and Morgan says, "I need to sit." Without protest we all grab hands and follow her to the back of the gym. We sit on the bleachers together about halfway up. Next to me Priah sweeps her hair off her neck. I give my own braids a little pat to make sure they're still holding, and am glad to find they are. Naeomi fans herself and then Priah, and Morgan leans back on her elbows, watching the crowd before us. Her face is even and cool, but when she catches me staring, she twists her mouth into this goofy grimace, stretching her lips in different directions, her eyes rolling back. We crack up.

The DJ starts a slow set then. The chaperones all take a few steps forward as couples immediately form and lean in together. I'm glad we're already sitting, so we don't look like we got driven off the dance floor just because we don't have slow-dance partners, like most of the masses now swarming to the bleachers around us. I've done a pretty good job so far of not really thinking about Disappearing Jake, but now I can't help it. I wonder where in the crowd he might be, if he's out there already somewhere, leaning on some other girl.

Ugh. Awful thought. So I watch Cameron twirl a chubby girl in purple tights and a scraggy tulle skirt around instead. A few other people start twirling too. We are all watching, not wanting to be. I look at Morgan and wonder if she wishes Cody were here, or is glad that he's not. She's been either quiet or exasperated whenever he's come up lately, which means, based on her track record, that a breakup is imminent, though I still haven't figured out if it'll come from him or her.

My eyes move to Priah. Of all of us, she's the one who wants a boyfriend most, and this makes her a prime candidate for getting wistful and sobby during the slow dances. There was this boy she had a "relationship" with back in Allegany, and even though they only kissed that one time, they kept up pretty well during our freshman year. After school started again in September, though, he stopped writing her back (Morgan and I figure he found someone actually in his own town, but whatever), and Priah got pretty melodramatic, especially since that was when Cara and Michael started getting serious for real. Priah's better now, but tonight I want to make sure she is still holding on to our shining happy dancing moments, instead of sinking into sad sighing. I want to catch her eye, to thank her for my fantastic hair, but as I'm trying I have to look away real fast because about ten feet beyond her is *him*. Jake. Jake Harper. Jake from Old United and Seymour High. Jake from Valentine's weekend. That Jake. Him.

Kisses. Sunshine.
Sunburn.

the summer of firsts and lasts

Three sisters.
One life-changing summer.

Terra Elan McVoy
author of *Pure*

Three sisters.
One unforgettable summer.

From Simon Pulse
Published by Simon & Schuster

From

the summer of firsts and lasts

by Terra Elan McVoy

Sneaking out to meet Brynn was so easy and uneventful and normal the first time, I almost forgot it was against the rules. When I see her tonight at karaoke, we don't talk about yesterday's thing at lunch at all. All that happens is that she plunks next to me, and then we laugh a ton together. When I hug her around the neck to tell her how awesome her Janis Joplin was, she only husks in my ear, "Tonight again."

And this time I'm way more excited than I am scared. Because of karaoke, though, it takes everyone else a lot longer to settle down to sleep, which makes me antsy. I'm a little less confident, too, since I can't tell if Natalie's really asleep or faking being asleep before *she* sneaks out. I am cat-burglar tiptoe quiet. But before I know it, I'm outside under the stars, figuring we're going up to the fire pit again to hang with whatever counselors are there tonight. Meaning James, I hope. Maybe we'll finally talk.

Brynn has other plans, though. She barely even says hey when I get to the boathouse, and just starts walking down to the dark edge of the lake, far away from all the cabins and their lights. Without a word, she shimmies off her pajama bottoms. She's wearing a boy-shorts swimsuit underneath.

"What are we doing?"

"Going for a swim, dummy. What does it look like?" She is half smiling.

"But I don't— I mean—"

"So swim in your pajamas." She whips her T-shirt off over her head, showing smooth white belly and too many ribs.

I go down and stick my foot in the water. It's chilly, but not totally freezing. It won't be comfortable at first, but I know I'll get used to it. But the air's too cool now to dry my pajamas before I get back to the cabin if I swim in them. And I am not very enthused about wearing wet underwear, which will then soak my pajamas, too. Taking things off and hanging them up will be a *way* too complicated chore when I'm trying to sneak back into my bunk. If I do this, I'm doing it au naturel.

"Or you can go back, it's cool," Brynn says, seeing me hesitate. Her voice is genuinely indifferent, not teasing or challenging. And I *could* go back. I kind of want to. But this is my last summer as a camper, and I don't want to be the girl who only heard about the crazy, rule-breaking things people did at camp, or saw them in the movies. I want to be the girl who *did* them. I want to be able to tell James about this whenever we *do* get to talk—to watch his face light up in surprise, imagining me out here. And naked. So off goes my top, and my sleep shorts and underpants are quick to follow. Brynn takes our clothes and shoves them in the seat of one of the kayaks chained to its rack.

"C'mon," she giggle-whispers. Something about how she sounds makes it seem like *she's* never done this before either.

The water is. Freezing. If it weren't midnight and I weren't breaking camp rules, I'd be squealing. Instead—somehow—I just grit my teeth and go under. It is so cold.

Hasn't stopped Brynn, though. When I come up, she's already knifing herself toward the floating dock in a freestyle that looks Olympic. I am not a swimmer. I mean, I can swim, and I like to, but we never got lessons or anything like that. My stroke is more like a turtle's.

By the time I make it out to the floating dock, I'm definitely warmer, and being in the water with no clothes on feels surprisingly good. You'd think, because a bathing suit sticks to you when you're wet and really isn't that much clothing to begin with, that there wouldn't be much of a difference, but there definitely—well, there just is. I almost don't want to get out, partly because in the water at least no one can see me. Gripping the ladder, I still get the feeling—even though it's impossible—someone might be looking out their cabin window, able to catch a glimpse.

But even Brynn can barely see me, and she's six feet away, though I'm sure my butt is white as chalk in whatever small moonlight there is. I haul myself up the ladder and sit down quick, bringing my knees up to my chest, wrapping my arms around myself and making sure my feet are blocking any view of my—you know. Since the three of us stopped taking showers together when Calla was about ten, I've really only been in my birthday suit when I'm by myself. Parts exposed, with different people, sure, but not, you know, the whole deal. I feel a little mad Brynn has her suit on. And a little proud I don't.

"You're a good swimmer," I say. My voice sounds loud though it isn't.

I think she shrugs.

"How come you're in Equestrian, and not Water Sports?"

"Their routine is messed up here," is all she answers.

"So you are on a team at home?"

"Yeah." She says it without any enthusiasm, but without disdain, either.

"I can never get that," I say after a minute. "The arms and the head thing."

"My favorite's the butterfly. It's hard, but that's why I like it. Not very many people are good at it."

And so that explains the serious shoulders she's got. Though for a swimmer I'd think she'd be more muscley and not so Skeletor. I decide not to ask her if she's won anything. I can't tell, from the way she's talking, if she wants me to be asking all these questions anyway, or not. Though this is the first time we've really hung out alone, she's half acting like we're already best friends who are completely comfortable with each other, half acting as though she doesn't care if I'm here.

Still, I have to talk to fill the quiet. "My mom took my little sister to those baby underwater classes—you know, where you throw babies in a pool and they just naturally hold their breath and paddle around?" I tell her.

She snorts.

"But it didn't make her some great swimmer. I mean, she swims, but none of us are real swimmers."

Mom said Daisy was the best baby in that whole class, though. She'd practically leap out of Mom's arms to get into that water. Sometimes if she got fussy we'd just fill up the tub and plop her in there, even when she was really small and couldn't even crawl or anything. She loved it. Why Mom never took me and Calla to those classes I don't know. When I asked her about it once she just cocked her head way over and frowned into space for a minute before she said, "You know, I have no idea. But it just never occurred to me for the two of you."

Brynn still doesn't say anything. Instead, I hear Saran Wrap rustling. I don't know what she's doing until there's a spark and a surprising flame, and then the fire goes up to her face and she inhales, holds it a minute, and then lets out a mossy-smoky breath.

"How can you be a swimmer and smoke?" I can't help blurting. She only chuckles. The orange dot that is the lit end of what she's smoking comes toward me.

"You want some?"

Which means it's pot. Which I should've figured anyway by the way it smelled. And it's stupid and embarrassing, but all I'm thinking is that if I smoke that with her, I won't be able to swim back. I picture myself naked, in the water, just floating there in the dark and unable to move my arms and legs, totally numb. I picture Calla having to come down to the lake to take away my pale, wet, bloated dead body.

"Where'd you get it?" I ask, stupid. The orange dot goes back to her and she takes another inhale.

"Brought it." Her voice is tight, like she's holding in her breath. The smoke that is somehow oilier and not as gross-smelling as regular cigarettes comes out at me again, and I feel like an idiot, sitting here with no clothes on, just some dumb girl Brynn brings along to keep an eye out while she smokes weed and drinks beers and hangs out with counselors and does whatever she wants. I don't even know why she's letting me tag around with her, until I realize I pretty much sought *her* out, not the other way around. She could probably care less whether I was here or not. She would do all these things with or without me. She isn't at all worried about making the swim back.

"Okay," I say.

"What?" The smoke comes out from her again. She coughs a little bit.

"Yeah, I want some, duh."

"Here," she says.

My fingers pinch around hers where she's holding the end of the joint out to me. It is warm, and a little bit damp. Shorter than I think it should be. The ember burns only an inch or so from my thumb. It's hard to get it close to my mouth without thinking I'm going to burn my nose off. I have to tilt my head a little. The nonburning end is mashed pretty flat, and when I suck in I'm not sure I'm going to get much, but then the ember glows brighter and a searing scratchiness goes into my throat, and my mouth fills up with this grossness that is the exact same taste as the smell of old flower water that's been in a vase for too long. Like the dumbasses smoking pot for the first time in the movies, I cough and cough and cough.

"Do it again," she says in her Johnny Cash voice. "It'll help."

So I take another hit, still scratchy and gross, still making me cough, but not as bad. My eyes are stinging with water. I hand it back to her.

She smokes the rest. I don't ask for any more and she doesn't offer. I just sit there, arms wrapped around myself and my butt starting to hurt from sitting on these hard planks. I watch her shape in the dark, and the orange dot growing and dimming and moving from her mouth to somewhere down around her lap, back and forth a few times before she's putting it out and there's the sound of Saran Wrap again. She tucks the lighter and the butt somewhere and stretches out on the planks of the dock, staring up.

I'm waiting for something to happen. For my head to swirl or to start giggling uncontrollably or my tongue to swell up or the skies to explode in comets or—something. But nothing does. Only my scratchy throat and kind of a warmish feeling in the front of my face. I take a deep breath and look up at the stars anyway, because stoned or not, they do look remarkable. And here I am, naked in the great outdoors and everything.

"My stepdad—" Brynn says out of nowhere. "He's who got me into swimming. At first I hated it. My mom wanted me to is why I did it, really. She wanted him and me to have something to do together, wanted me to be active. He would get up really early to go to work before everyone else so he could leave at three to take me to swim lessons. I was, I think, ten. I wasn't fat or anything, but when I started swimming I got really . . . *skinny*. And by sixth grade I was wearing a zero. Sure, in my school *most* of the sixth-grade girls wore zeros. But by seventh, eighth, all of them started getting boobs and hips and puberty fat and all that. And me, with all my swimming, I was a total board—flat. And you know how girls are always made fun of for having no chest?"

I hear her head turn on the wood planks as she looks over at me. I grunt a kind of yes, to keep her going mostly, to see what she's going to say.

"Well. I didn't care. I wanted to swim harder, more often, more. I wanted to keep all the girl fat off me I could. And even though now I go to this school that has a pool, like, three blocks away, one I can walk to and don't need a ride to anymore, my stepdad's still going in to work early, still coming to my practices, all my meets."

She's quiet for a minute. "At first I hated him so much. And my mom. And he knew that, and he probably hated me for a while too, this total brat little bitch, but he just kept driving me to those swim lessons all those years and keeps on watching and clapping and taking us out for pizza sometimes afterward and buying my coach a beer— just smiling and happy and pounding me on the shoulder like I'm his real kid or something."

She's quiet, and I don't say anything. I've stopped being cold. I've stopped feeling my sore butt. I've even kind of forgotten that we're actually at camp, instead of just in some private dark place that is totally our own. Which is what makes me remember, suddenly, that we *are* at camp. And I'm out here on the dock, naked, and I just smoked pot for the first time, and Brynn, this girl I barely know— this tough, shocking girl—is out here with me being, in her own way, completely naked too. And I think, how can this be against the rules? How can something like this be against camp policy? Because this—*this*—is exactly what camp should be all about.

About the Author

Terra Elan McVoy started writing poetry seriously in sixth grade, just after she found a volume of e. e. cummings on her mom's bookshelf. Since then, most of her life has centered around reading and writing, from managing an independent children's bookstore to teaching writing classes, and even answering fan mail for Captain Underpants (though she spent some time as a bakery counter girl too). Terra lives and works in the same Atlanta neighborhood where *After the Kiss* and her first novel, *Pure*, are set. To learn more about Terra's life, visit terraelan.com.

Jammed full of surprises!

VISIT US AT WWW.LIPSMACKERLOUNGE.COM!

Some secrets are worth keeping.

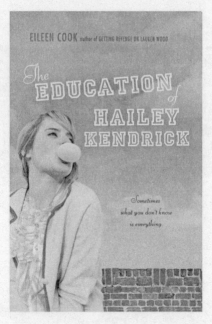

Don't miss these other funny reads from
Eileen Cook:

siMonTEEN

Simon & Schuster's **Simon Teen**
e-newsletter delivers current updates on
the hottest titles, exciting sweepstakes, and
exclusive content from your favorite authors.

Visit **TEEN.SimonandSchuster.com** to
sign up, post your thoughts, and find out what
every avid reader is talking about!

  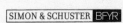